LABYRINTH

BILL PRONZINI

ST. MARTIN'S PRESS, NEW YORK

Library of Congress Cataloging in Publication Data

Pronzini, Bill.
  Labyrinth.

  I. Title.
PZ4.P9653Lab   [PS3566.R67]   813'.5'4   79-22856
ISBN 0-312-46352-9

This one is for the memory of *Black Mask, Blue Book, Golden Fleece, Green Ghost Detective, Red Star Mystery,* and all the other magazines of the colorful pulp era.

ONE

The dead girl lay in a twisted sprawl, like something broken and carelessly discarded, among the reeds and bushes that grew along the edge of Lake Merced.

I could see her from where I stood alone on the embankment thirty feet above, and I could watch the movements of the half-dozen Homicide cops and forensic people who were down there with her. One of the cops was Eberhardt. He knew I was waiting up here, but he had not paid any attention to me since my arrival a couple of minutes ago; he wasn't ready yet to tell me why I had been summoned out of a sound sleep at seven A.M. to the place where a young girl had died.

It was a cold gray Wednesday morning in November, and the wind blowing in across Skyline carried the heavy smells of salt and rain. Pockets of mist clung to the reeds and trees and underbrush around the lake shore, giving the concrete pedestrian causeway at the south end an oddly insubstantial look, like an optical illusion. The whole area seemed desolate at this hour, but that was illusion too: Lake Merced sits in the southwestern corner of San Francisco, not far from the ocean, and is surrounded by public and private golf courses, upper- and middleclass residential areas, San Francisco State College, and the Fleishhacker Zoo.

It had been awhile since my last trip out here. But when I was on the cops a number of years ago I had come to the lake at least once a month, sometimes with Eberhardt, because the police pistol range was nearby to the west. Another inspector had had a small sailboat in those days, moored over at the Harding Boat House, and if the weather was good the three of us would take it out on Saturdays or Sundays. Lake Merced is bigger than you would expect an in-city body of water to be, and because of its location, removed from the tourist areas downtown and along the Bay, it's a recreation area pretty much reserved for the natives.

Behind me I heard another vehicle come wheeling in off Lake Merced Boulevard. I turned, saw that it was a city ambulance, and watched it maneuver to a stop among the blue-and-whites and unmarked police sedans—and my car—that were strewn across the wide dirt parking area opposite Brotherhood Way. Two attendants in white uniforms got out and opened up the rear doors. While they were doing that, a coroner's car swung in and joined the pack; the guy who stepped out of it, carrying a medical bag, came over and stopped beside me.

"Where is it?" he said, as if he were asking about a tree stump or a piece of machinery. He seemed to think I was one of the Homicide inspectors. "Down there?"

"Yeah," I said. "Down there."

"Sorry I'm late." But he did not sound sorry; he only sounded aggrieved. "Goddamn car wouldn't start."

I had nothing to say to that. He shrugged, pulled a face, gave me a short nod, and began to make his way down to where the dead girl was.

I looked away again. The knots of people along the bicycle

paths that flanked the parking area—college kids from S.F. State, residents of the lakeview townhouses down the way, reporters and TV-remote crews—seemed to be getting larger; cars crawled along Lake Merced Boulevard, filled wih eager gawking faces. Ghouls, all of them. There were half a dozen uniformed patrolmen working crowd control in the area, but the cops knew and I knew that the crowds would not be dispersed until after the body was taken away.

The cold bite of the wind was making my eyes water. I rubbed at them with the back of one hand, reburied the hand in my topcoat pocket, and bunched the material tight around me. Filaments of black, like veins, had started to form in the overcast sky; we were going to have rain pretty soon. I considered waiting inside my car, where I could use the heater to chase some of the morning chill—but before I could make up my mind to do that, Eberhardt's voice called my name from below.

I stepped back to the edge of the embankment and saw him peering up at me, beckoning. "Okay," he said, "you can come on down."

So I let out a breath and picked my way along the slope, using the vegetation there to keep my balance on the wet grass. When I got to where Eberhardt was, he turned without saying anything and led me to the girl's body.

"Take a look," he said then, "tell me if you recognize her."

She was lying on her stomach, but her head was canted around so that most of her face was visible toward the lake. There was one hole on the left side of her forehead, black-edged and caked with dried blood, and a second just below the collarbone. Shot twice, with what was probably a small caliber weapon judging from the size of the entry wounds and because there did not seem to be any exit wounds. She had been young, maybe still in her teens, and she had been attractive; you could tell that even with her features blanked and frozen in death. Long dark hair, pug nose, sprinkling of freckles across her cheekbones. Wearing a suede coat, tennis shoes, jeans, and one of those football-type jerseys, red and white, with the number forty-nine on it.

I had never seen her before.

My stomach coiled up as I looked at her. After a couple of seconds I swung around and stood staring out over the wind-wrinkled surface of the lake. I had seen death before—too much death, too many bodies torn and ravaged by violence—but each time was like the first: a hollow feeling under the breastbone, the taste of bile, a sense of sadness and awe. I had never learned to inure myself to it, never become jaded or detached enough, the way some cops did, to treat it as an abstract.

But this time I felt something else, too—a kind of dull empty rage. A young girl like that, robbed of life before she had much of a chance to live it. Why? Where was the sense in such a brutal act? No matter what she might have done to someone, no matter what she might have been, she could not have deserved to die this way.

Beside me Eberhardt said, "Well?" His voice was sharp and gruff, and I knew him well enough after thirty years to understand that the girl's death had touched him too.

I shook my head. "I don't know her, Eb."

"You sure?"

"I'm sure."

"All right. We'll talk up top. I'm finished here."

He asked the assistant coroner if he could release the body, got an affirmative nod, and the two of us climbed back up to the parking area. I watched him gesture to the ambulance attendants and then take out one of his flame-blackened briar pipes and clamp it between his teeth. He was my age, fifty-two, and an odd contrast of sharp angles and smooth blunt planes: square forehead, sharp nose and chin, thick and blocky upper body, long legs and angular hands. His usual expression was one of sourness and cynicism—a false reflection of what he was like inside—but now his face had a dark, brooding cast. I wondered if he were thinking about his niece, the one who was not much older than the dead girl by the lake.

When the ambulance attendants came past us with the stretcher and disappeared below, Eberhardt said to me, "Her name was Christine Webster. Mean anything to you?"

"No."

"We found her purse in one of those bushes on the slope," he said. "Address on her driver's license is Edgewood Avenue, up by the U.C. Med Center. She was twenty years old and a student at S.F. State; student I.D. card in her wallet, along with the license."

"None of that rings any bells," I said.

"You working on anything connected with the college?"

"No. I'm not working on anything at all right now."

"You know anybody up around the Med Center?"

"I don't think so, no. Look, Eb—"

"Not much else in her purse. Except one thing."

"What thing?"

"One of your business cards," he said.

"So that's it."

"That's it. Kind of funny for a girl that young to be carrying around a private eye's business card, don't you think?"

"I think. Christ."

"But you're positive you never saw or heard from her?"

"I'd remember if I had."

"What about phone calls or letters from unidentified women. Anything like that recently?"

"No. I'm sorry, no."

"You hand out many of those cards?"

"A fair amount, sure," I said. "Insurance companies, lawyers, bail bondsmen, skip-trace clients, friends, casual acquaintances—hell, I must have distributed a thousand or more over the past few years."

There were sounds on the slope behind us, and we both turned to look as the ambulance attendants struggled up with the stretcher. When they got to the top and started past us, a ripple of movement and sound passed through the watchers along Lake Merced Boulevard. You could almost see them all leaning forward for a better look, even though the shell of Christine Webster was just a small shapeless mound beneath the sheet and restraining straps.

Eberhardt said, "Bastards."

"Yeah."

He got a little box of wooden matches out of his pocket, hunched over to shield his hands from the wind, and used four of the matches to get his pipe lighted. "Okay," he said then. "She picked up your card somehow, and maybe she was planning to contact you, but for whatever reason she never did. The point is, is there a connection between that and her death?"

I had been wondering the same thing. The idea of it bothered me; I had not known the girl existed until this morning, when she no longer did exist, and yet the fact that she'd had my business card was a thread linking her life and mine. If there was a connection, and if she *had* come to me about her problem, could I have done anything to prevent her murder? But that kind of thinking never got you anywhere. I had allowed myself to indulge in it in the past and I had promised myself, for a number of reasons, that I was not going to do it anymore.

For the sake of argument I said, "It could be she had the card as a gag. You know, the way kids do—flash it on her friends, make up some kind of story to go with it."

"Maybe."

I stared over at where the attendants were loading her body into the ambulance. "Could it have been robbery?" I asked. "Or attempted rape?"

"It wasn't robbery," Eberhardt said. "There're thirty-three dollars in her wallet and a gold engagement ring on one of her fingers. And it doesn't figure to be rape; she wasn't molested or otherwise abused."

"Street shooting?"

"Possible but not likely. She lived way the hell up on Edgewood, and with Thanksgiving coming up there won't be any night classes at the college for the next couple of weeks. Seems doubtful she'd have been wandering around here alone at night. Coroner's rough estimate as to time of death is between nine P.M. and midnight."

"She could have been killed somewhere else," I said. "Or picked up somewhere else and forced into a car and brought here."

6

"Uh-uh. See that old blue Mustang down at the end there? Belongs to Christine Webster. Lab boys have been over it already; no bloodstains or anything else that figures to be important. The way it looks, she either drove here to meet someone or came willingly with the person who shot her."

"Anything in the area that might point to the killer?"

"Nothing. She was shot at close range with a small caliber handgun—.25 or .32, probably. Then she either fell down the slope or was rolled down it after she was dead. College kid out jogging at six-thirty spotted the body and called us. That's all we know for sure so far."

The ambulance started up and eased out onto the street. The rubberneckers all turned to watch it fade out of sight toward the campus. End of show. They began to drift away singly and in small groups.

Eberhardt said, "So that's that for now. You can take off, *paisan*. I'll let you know if we turn up anything definite."

"Do that, huh? A thing like this . . ."

"Yeah, I know," he said. "Go on, get out of here. I'll be in touch."

I went over to my car and managed to get inside and away from there without being hassled by the media types that were still hanging around. The sky had grown darker; droplets of rain began to spatter against the windshield. I could still feel the chill of the wind and I turned the heater up as high as it would go.

Twenty years old, I thought, and somebody shot her dead. My business card in her purse and somebody shot her dead.

I stayed cold all the way downtown.

TWO

It was after nine when I reached the Tenderloin and parked
my car in the Taylor and Eddy lot, not far from where I have
my office. I thought about going into a nearby greasy spoon for
some breakfast, but I had no appetite; the image of the dead
girl was still sharp in my mind. Instead I locked the car and
hustled straight up the hill on Taylor.

The rain kept on coming down, alternating between a drizzle
and a fine mist, and the wind was gusty enough to slap the
coattails around my legs. At this hour and in this weather the
streets were pretty much empty. The dark wet sky made them
and the old buildings look dingier and more unappealing than
usual. Even the faint pervading smell of garbage seemed
stronger.

The Tenderloin used to be, and on the surface still was, a
section of lunchrooms and seedy bars and secondhand book-

stores; of low-rent apartment buildings and cheap hotels inhabited by transients, senior citizens with small pensions, nonviolent drifters and the Runyonesque street characters that were as much an institution in San Francisco as they once were in New York. It used to have character, the way Broadway-Times Square did in the old days, and you could walk its streets in relative safety. But in the past couple of decades it had changed—had lost all of its flavor and taken on instead a kind of desperate sleaziness. The transients and senior citizens were still there, but the street characters had been replaced by drug addicts and drug pushers, small-time thugs, fancy-dressed pimps and hard-eyed whores. You walked on Eddy or Mason or Turk or lower Taylor these days, and you saw porno bookstores and movie houses spread out like garish weeds; you saw men and women openly buying and selling smack, coke, any other kind of drug you can name; you saw spaced-out kids, drunks sleeping it off in doorways, elderly people with frightened eyes watchful for purse-snatchers and muggers because the Tenderloin has the highest crime rate in the city.

I asked myself again why I didn't, for Christ's sake, move my office to a better neighborhood. Business had not been all that good recently, and maybe part of the reason was my location. Who wants to put his trust in a private investigator with an office on the fringe of the Tenderloin?

Moving made good sense—but the problem was, I couldn't really afford to move. The rent in my building was reasonable enough, even though the landlord was making noises about kicking it up again; the price of an office in a more respectable area was beyond my means. Besides which, I had occupied this one ever since I left the cops and went out on my own fourteen years ago; I liked it there, I felt comfortable there.

So I was not going to move and that was that. Just keep on toughing it out, I told myself. Hell, you've had plenty of practice at toughing things out, right? Particularly in the past year and a half.

When I entered my building and started across to the elevator I noticed the white of an envelope showing inside my mailbox.

There were envelopes inside all the other boxes, too. Uh-oh, I thought, because it was too early for the mail; and there was only one other person with access to the boxes. I opened mine up and took out the envelope: my name hand-written on the front, the building owner's name and address rubber-stamped in the upper left-hand corner. Greetings from your friendly landlord.

I said something under my breath, stuffed the envelope into my coat pocket, and took the elevator up to the third floor. My office was cold; and it still seemed to retain the faint smell of stale cigarettes. I had not smoked a cigarette in seventeen months, ever since finding out about the lesion on my left lung, but I had averaged two packs a day before that. Maybe the walls and furnishings had permanently absorbed the smoke odor. But probably it was just a ghost smell—a similar kind of thing to the imagined sensations an amputee feels once he has lost an arm or a leg. When you live with something for most or all of your life you never quite adjust to the fact that it's gone.

The first thing I did was to check my answering machine. Up until the beginning of this year, I had subscribed to a regular service; but then inflation had forced them to raise their rates, and that in turn had forced me to go out and buy the machine. It was something I should have done years ago, maybe, except that I had an old-fashioned outlook on the conventions of the private detecting business.—I suppose because I identified strongly with the fictional eyes and cops in the pulp magazines I had read and collected for more than thirty years. I had always wanted to emulate the Spades and Marlowes and Race Williamses, and if that was childish and self-deluding, as a woman named Erika Coates had once claimed, then so be it. It was my life and the only person I had to justify my feelings to was myself.

I did not expect to find anything on the machine: I list my home number on my cards and in the phone book in case anybody decides on the weekend that he needs a private investigator, reasonable rates, strict confidence at all times. But I had had at least one call because the little window on one corner had a round white spot in it. I worked the controls and listened to my voice play back the message I had recorded. Then a woman's businesslike voice said, "Yes, this is Mrs. Laura Nichols. Would you please call me as soon as possible?" She gave a number, repeated it—and that was all.

I wrote the name and number down on a pad. Then I went over and fiddled with the steam radiator until the pipes began banging and thumping. Took my coffeepot into the alcove, emptied out the dregs of last Friday's coffee, filled it with fresh water from the sink tap in there, and put it on the hotplate to heat. Morning ritual.

Sitting at the desk, I opened the letter from my landlord. It said what I expected: my rent was being raised thirty dollars a month, effective December 1. No explanation, no apology. Nice. Some time ago the California voters had passed the Jarvis-Gann tax-reform initiative, Proposition 13, which gave property owners a 60 percent tax cut per annum; and ever since the governor had made a lot of noise about owners passing on some of that savings to renters. Result: a thirty-dollar increase on an office in the goddamn Tenderloin.

I threw the letter into the wastebasket. The thing with Christine Webster and my business card had already made it a lousy Monday; this was just the icing. Well, maybe Mrs. Laura Nichols, whoever she was, had something positive to offer. Like a job. I had not worked at anything in five days and I needed both the activity and the money.

So I pulled the phone over, dialed the number I had written down. While I waited I sat looking at the poster blow-up of a 1932 *Black Mask* cover that I had tacked up on one wall. It was not exactly appropriate for a business office, but I liked it and that was what counted. Eberhardt, on one of his infrequent visits here, had said that it made the place look like something out of an old Bogart movie. Me and Bogie and Sam Spade—

The same businesslike female voice said hello in my ear. I asked, "Mrs. Nichols?" and she said yes and I identified myself.

"Oh, yes—good. Thank you for calling."

"How can I help you, Mrs. Nichols?"

11

"Are you free to accept a confidential job? It would be on a full-time basis for at least two weeks."

"Yes, ma'am. Depending on what it involves, of course."

"It's a rather delicate family matter, concerning my brother. I'd prefer not to discuss the details on the phone, but it isn't anything unseemly. We can discuss it at my home, if you don't mind driving out. I'm sure it will be worth your time."

"When would you like me to come?"

"As soon as possible," she said. "The address is 2519 Twenty-Fifth Avenue North. In Sea Cliff."

I raised an eyebrow. Sea Cliff is a synonym for money in San Francisco; you don't live there unless your yearly income is around six figures. "I can be there within the hour," I said.

"Fine. I'll expect you."

She rang off, and I cradled the handset, gazing again at the *Black Mask* poster. Full-time job for at least two weeks, working for a lady in Sea Cliff? It was the kind of thing that always happened to the pulp private eyes, but that happened to me about as often as a woman who said "yes" on the first date. So there figured to be a catch in it somewhere that I was not going to like. The last time I had worked for a rich client—one of the few times in my career—I had wound up in the hospital with a knife wound in my belly. I still had the scars, one you could see and one you couldn't.

But then, why expect the worst? Maybe it was all going to be fine; maybe for a change I was going to get a break. I stood up and poured myself a quick cup of coffee. Then I locked the office and went down and out to pick up my car.

THREE

Twenty-five nineteen Twenty-Fifth Avenue North turned out to be a massive beige stucco house separated from its neighbors by a lot of bright green lawn. Its architecture was so old-California Spanish that it looked as if it belonged in Los Angeles instead of San Francisco: red-tile roof, decorative wrought-iron balconies framing all of the windows, front portico with a black-beam archway, wall patterns here and there done in four colors of mosaic tile. There were even mosaic tile inlays in the series of terraced steps that led up from the street.

I parked in front and climbed the steps. The rain had stopped, but the morning was still damp and dismal-gray with overcast; the wind here was blustery, knife-edged. Behind and on both sides of the house you could see the broad choppy sweep of the ocean and the entrance to the Bay, and through the low clouds the towers of the Golden Gate Bridge, the brown hills of Marin, the cliffs at Land's End. The view would be spectacular on a clear day, which was what made the Sea Cliff area prime real estate; even now it was pretty impressive.

A big brass knocker shaped like a lion's head sat in the center of the front door, but I found a doorbell button and used that instead. Chimes sounded faintly inside, faded to silence. Another ten seconds went by before a peephole above the knocker opened and an amber-colored eye peered out at me. A woman's voice, different from the one on the phone, said "Yes?" in the tone people use on door-to-door salesmen.

I gave my name and added that Mrs. Nichols was expecting me.

Pause. "You're that private detective."

"Yes, that's right."

Another pause. Then the voice said, "Just a moment," and there was the scraping of a lock, the door opened, and I was looking at a tall slender woman in her early twenties. She had fine, pale-blonde hair cut short in the style we used to call shag and a pale sensitive face dominated by high cheekbones. The amber eyes were wide and striking. She wore one of those long button-down skirts that are supposed to be popular now, a white blouse and a little black knit vest.

"Come in, please."

I went in. She shut the door, locked it again, waited for me to give her my coat, and then hung it away in a closet—all without smiling, speaking, or even looking at me. We went down a dark hall and through another of those Spanish archways into a living room. The floors were tiled and carpetless; my heels clicked so loudly that it made me a little self-conscious, the kind of feeling you get when you walk through a church or maybe a museum.

The young woman gestured to a large bulky sofa. "I'll tell my mother you're here," she said.

"Thank you."

She went away through the arch. I sat on the sofa with my hat on my knees and looked at the room. The Spanish effect seemed overdone, as if the people who lived here were trying too hard to create an atmosphere of old-world gentility. The antique furniture included a refectory table, a pigeonhole desk, several big chairs with flat wood arms and bare wood backs; a massive rococo chandelier hung from the ceiling. On the far side a set of narrow glass doors gave access to a patio that had a mosaic tile floor and a lot of bushes and plants growing out of brown urns. It was all dark and ponderous, a little depressing. There was not much color anywhere; even the old paintings on the walls were somber-hued. About the only modern things in the room were a stereo unit and a typewriter on the desk, and they seemed out of place.

I sat there for about two minutes. There was no sound anywhere, not even the ticking of a clock. Then I heard steps on the hall tiles, and got on my feet as a large handsome woman in her late forties or early fifties appeared at the arch. She came through it like a stockholder entering a board room: poised, purposeful, self-assured. A tailored green pants suit set off carefully coiffed blonde hair and the same amber eyes as her daughter, just a little darker under long curling lashes. There was a diamond as big as a grape on the ring finger of her left hand.

No smile from her either. She said, "I'm Laura Nichols," and offered me her hand, then shook mine in the same businesslike way. Her eyes went over me in frank appraisal, but there was nothing in them or on her face to tell what sort of impression she was getting. She asked me to sit down, and when I did she went over and arranged herself in one of the heavy wooden chairs.

"Would you care for coffee? Tea?"

"Thanks, no."

She nodded as if she approved of my answer. "Then I'll get directly to the point," she said. Her enunciation was careful and precise; I had the feeling that everything she did would be with care and precision. "I've asked you here because of my brother, Martin Talbot. He's had a very unfortunate experience, you see."

"Oh?"

"Yes. Two nights ago, while he was driving back from a Los

15

Angeles business trip, he fell asleep at the wheel of his car near South San Francisco. The car veered into another lane, struck another car and caused it to spin into an overpass abutment. Martin wasn't hurt, miraculously enough, but one of the two people in the other car was killed."

A very unfortunate experience, she'd said. That was some way of putting it.

Mrs. Nichols went on, "The driver of the second car, a man named Victor Carding, also escaped serious injury; it was his wife who died. Later, in the hospital, my brother insisted on seeing Carding and spoke to him alone for a minute or two. During that time the man called Martin a murderer, threatened his life, and then tried to attack him. Two interns came in and restrained him just in time."

"You're afraid Carding might try to carry out his threat—is that it?"

"Yes. He's due to be released from the hospital today."

"Have you talked to the police?"

"Of course. As soon as Martin told me."

"And?"

"They seem to feel there's nothing to worry about. When they spoke to Carding he told them he couldn't remember threatening Martin or trying to attack him. He claims not to hold my brother responsible for what happened."

"Well, that's probably the case," I said. "People do and say things in shock and grief that they don't really mean."

"Perhaps. But we can't be certain of that. Carding is a construction worker, a common laborer; there's no telling what a man like that is capable of."

Common laborer, I thought. Why do people like her always use the word "common" as if there was some social stigma attached to being a blue collar worker? Christ, we're *all* laborers of one kind or another.

I said, "What does your brother think?"

"That Carding would be justified if he chose to seek revenge."

"I'm not sure I follow that, Mrs. Nichols."

16

"You would have to know my brother to fully understand," she said. "He's an unusual man."

"In what way?"

"In many ways. Our father was a banker, quite well-to-do, and when he passed on he left Martin and me a substantial sum of money. Martin refused to accept his share of the estate; it was his belief that he had no right to the inheritance because he hadn't earned the money himself. He worked his way through college, received a degree in electrical engineering, and proceeded to follow his own path in life. He has been moderately successful, I'll admit—"

She broke off because her daughter, silent as a wraith, had appeared in the archway. Mrs. Nichols gave her a somewhat annoyed glance and said, "What is it, Karen?"

"Do you mind if I come in?"

"I'm discussing a business matter, dear."

"Yes—with a private detective. About Uncle Martin. I've a right to know what you're planning, why you want a detective."

Mrs. Nichols pursed her lips and looked at me. The look said that children really could be difficult at times, couldn't they? I kept my expression stoic and attentive; I had no opinion on the subject of children. And none I cared to show about a mother who appeared to think of her twenty-odd-year-old daughter as a child.

"Oh, all right," she said to Karen. "Come in, if you must. You won't leave me alone, I suppose, until you do find out."

The girl came inside and sat on one of the chairs at the refectory table—with her knees clasped together and her posture erect and her hands folded in her lap. I wondered if there were still such things as finishing schools. If so, Karen had no doubt been sent to one—whether she wanted to attend or not.

All of Mrs. Nichols' attention settled on me again. She said, "As I was about to say, my brother is also the most moral man I have ever known. He lives by the strictest code of behavior imaginable; what is right is right, what is wrong is wrong, and there are absolutely no gray areas or extenuating circumstances.

17

I'm sure that's why he's still a bachelor at forty-four; he simply never found a woman who measured up to his standards."

I said, "He feels guilt over the accident, then?"

"That is an understatement. He has barely slept since it happened, eaten almost nothing, and hasn't gone back to his job or even left his house except for short walks around the neighborhood. He considers himself to be just what Carding called him: A murderer. His 'negligence'—his word, not mine—caused the death of another human being. He even expressed the desire to stand trial for manslaughter; thank God that isn't legally possible. The point is, if Victor Carding attempted to harm him, I doubt Martin would try to prevent it. He is altogether on Carding's side on the matter, if you see what I mean."

"Yes," I said, "I see what you mean."

"In view of that, it's my duty to have him protected. That's why I called you."

I frowned at her. "You want me to act as his bodyguard?"

"Essentially, yes."

"Why would he consent, feeling as he does?"

"He wouldn't, if he knew about it."

"*If* he knew about it?"

"Martin lives across the street from Stern Grove; you can see his house from inside the park, front and back. What I want you to do is watch the house for any sign of Carding and also to follow Martin whenever he goes out walking. He's a compulsive walker, you see; and of course he refuses to ever drive a car again."

I knew there'd be a catch, I thought. Damn, I knew it.

I shifted on my chair. I had been offered a lot of different jobs over the years, not a few of them of the screwball variety, but this was something new out of left field. Bodyguard-from-a-distance. Christ. People get the damnedest ideas into their heads.

Karen apparently had a similar reaction. She said, "I don't think that's a very good idea, mother."

"Don't you, now?"

"No. Victor Carding isn't going to come after Uncle Martin;

I don't believe that. But even if he did, what could this man do about it?"

"I'm afraid your daughter's right, Mrs. Nichols," I said. "Carding could just ring the doorbell and attack your brother when he answers; there wouldn't be time enough for me to stop him. Or he could let Carding inside, of his own free will. In that case I couldn't just break in—not without a hundred-percent certainty that an attempted murder was about to take place. I'm a private investigator, not a police officer. I don't have any more rights than you or any other private citizen."

"Don't you suppose I'm aware of all that?" Mrs. Nichols said. Her voice was cool, almost patronizing, as if she felt now that she was dealing with a pair of "children" instead of just one. "But there *might* be something you could do. You *might* be able to prevent another tragedy. If no one watches over Martin, then no one can prevent anything from happening in an emergency."

She more or less had a point. But I said, "You'd want me to keep this watch on your brother for at least two weeks?"

"Yes. If nothing were to happen in that time, I would feel satisfied that Carding's threat was meaningless."

"Would you want a full twenty-four hour vigil?"

"Certainly."

"That's a three-man job," I said. "I'd have to hire two other operatives and pay them full salary."

Karen said, "You know what he's saying, don't you, mother? It would cost a small fortune—"

"I know what it will cost." There was frost in the lady's voice now; she did not like to be argued with. "The expense is of little importance. Your uncle's safety is all that matters."

"I still don't think it's a good idea—"

"I don't care *what* you think, young woman. And I'll thank you to be quiet from now on or else leave the room."

Karen glanced at me, looked back at her mother, and then lowered her eyes to her folded hands. I thought I saw her lips form words, thought I recognized what they were; but it was difficult to be sure with her head bowed and the lighting in there. If I was right, though, the words explained a good deal about her side of this mother-daughter relationship.

What she seemed to say was, "'Stubborn old bitch.'"

Mrs. Nichols asked me, "Do you have any more questions or observations?"

"No, I don't think so."

"Well, then? Will you accept the job?"

I thought it over. It was screwball, all right. Judging from what she had told me about Martin Talbot, he needed the services of a psychiatrist a lot more than those of a private detective. But if the surveillance did last at least two weeks, the kind of money involved would pay my groceries, the rent on my flat, and the just-raised rent on my office for the next few months. You can turn down a prospective client when there's a question of ethics; but when you're dealing with sensitivities, and when you have to worry about making ends meet, it's no damned contest at all.

"Yes, ma'am," I said. "I'll accept the job."

FOUR

Martin Talbot's house was located on the corner of Twenty-first Avenue and Wawona, directly across from the north-side entrance to Stern Grove—a fourteen-block-long park and recreation area on the west side of the city, a mile or so from San Francisco State College and Lake Merced. It was a modest stucco affair, boxy-looking, painted white with a red tile roof, that stood shoulder-to-shoulder with its immediate neighbors. In front were a tiny patch of trimmed lawn, a brick staircase, a built-in garage under what would probably be the living room windows. Behind the house was a tiny fenced yard; you would be able to see the side gate and at least part of the rear porch from within the park.

It was after two o'clock when I got there. I parked my car on Wawona, facing east, and entered the park through the gate in its cyclone border fence. The rain had not started up again, but it was in the air and in the bite of the wind. Nobody else was out and around that I could see; the rolling lawns, the kid-sized soccer field, the short driving range for golfers to practice their chip shots, the sunken putting green, all looked deserted.

There were no benches to sit on, but in this weather it would not have mattered if there had been; it was too damned cold to sit out in the open. I wandered around for a time on the wet grass, to refamiliarize myself with the landscape and to see how far I could go east and west and still have a clear view of Talbot's house. Cars drifted by now and then and there was a steady whisper-and-rumble of traffic over on Nineteenth Avenue; otherwise it was a pretty quiet area. You could even hear water dripping off the eucalyptus and other trees that lined the north rim of Stern Grove's deep, wide central grotto.

When my nose and ears began to burn I went back out to sit in the car. What I wanted more than anything right then was some hot coffee. I wished I had thought to buy a thermos and fill it from the pot in my office; I had driven there after leaving Sea Cliff, to make some calls and check my answering machine, and there were stores in the vicinity where I could have got a thermos. I made a mental note to do that tomorrow, before I came back out here.

I started the engine, put the heater on full blast until I was warm again. Then I opened up a 1943 issue of *Black Mask*. But trying to read on a surveillance is not much of an idea; you can't concentrate because you have to keep glancing up after every paragraph or two in order to stay alert. At the end of fifteen minutes I gave it up—and just sat there.

Nothing happened over at the Talbot house. Nothing happened anywhere, except that a woman with a poodle on a leash came walking down Wawona behind me, crossed the street in front of my car, and entered the park. She gave me a curious glance as she passed, the kind that meant she was wondering what I was doing there.

I sighed a little. Curious neighbors, like as not, were going to present a problem eventually; you *could* run a two-week, round-the-clock stakeout in a residential area without arousing suspicion, but the odds were against it. Both Bert Thomas and Milo Petrie—a pair of retired cops who worked part-time as guards and field operatives—had mentioned the fact to me when I called them from my office. They had been willing to take the other two eight-hour shifts, but neither of them figured the job to last the full two weeks. Which made three of us. Sooner or later one of the neighbors was liable to get suspicious enough and worried enough to make a police complaint, and that would be the end of it. Not because the police would hassle us, although they might if there was pressure applied; there was nothing illegal in a surveillance conducted by licensed private investigators. But because word would get around the neighborhood, and if we tried to keep on watching the Talbot house, the whole thing would turn into a circus full of rumor-mongering and gawking citizens. And that wouldn't do anybody any good, least of all Martin Talbot.

A crazy damned job. But I was committed to it now, for as long as it lasted. I shook my head and wondered why I never got the kind of cases the pulp private eyes did. No slinky blondes with bedroom eyes and horny dispositions. No stolen jewels or missing heiresses. No danger and intrigue among the decadent rich. Well, maybe I ought to consider myself fortunate. If I never got laid by my lady clients, I also never got hit on the head or had shoot-outs with hired gunmen in dark alleys. Better a nice safe dull stakeout like this than a knife wound in the belly. Or being trapped in a mine cave-in in the Mother Lode, which was another thing that had happened to me on a past case.

Over in the park, next to where her poodle was squatting and soiling the grass, the woman stood peering in my direction again. So I got out of the car and hoisted the hood and pretended to fiddle around with the engine. That made her lose interest in me; when she came out a couple of minutes later she passed by without a glance. And she did not look back as she followed the poodle along the far sidewalk.

I waited until she turned out of sight on Twenty-third Avenue; then I closed the hood and got back into the front seat. And sat there again, trying not to look at my watch every minute or two.

It was only a little past three-thirty: four and a half hours to go on my abbreviated shift. We had settled on a regular timetable beginning at eight tonight—Bert Thomas would be on from then until four A.M., Milo Petrie from four until noon, and me from noon until eight P.M. Which gave me the best of the three shifts, but they didn't mind and the prerogatives were mine.

My mind fidgeted from one thought to another, the way minds do when you're just sitting somewhere and not doing anything with your hands. One of the things it kept coming back to was the murder of Christine Webster. I had called Eberhardt while I was in the office, but he had no further information to give me. The city coroner had not finished his post-mortem examination at that time, and the Homicide inspectors assigned to the case—Klein and Logan—had only just begun interviewing the dead girl's friends and relatives.

Why did Christine have my business card when they found her? That and other questions kept on nagging at me. What kind of trouble had she been in that would make her consider seeing a private detective? Did the trouble have anything to do with her murder? If she'd had the card for any length of time, why hadn't she called me or come to talk to me?

Twenty years old. Dead. Murdered.

Why? Who and why?

I had a vivid mental image of her lying among the reeds and bushes, all bloody and twisted, and the anger cut at me again and made me feel restless. But there was nothing I could do about her—a dead girl I had never known. Nothing I could do about anything at the moment. Just sit and wait, sit and wait—

Martin Talbot appeared on the small front porch of his house.

I sat up straighter, watching him as he started down the brick staircase. I knew for sure it was Talbot because Laura Nichols had given me his description earlier, along with one of Victor Carding that she had pried out of her brother. Large, fair-skinned man with fanshell ears and close-cropped, wheat-colored hair. Wearing a tweed overcoat today, no hat or muffler. He turned toward me at the sidewalk and crossed the street ten yards ahead of my car, moving with a mechanical stride, head held stiff and motionless, like an automaton activated by remote control. Even at that distance, I could see that his expression was almost masklike, without animation.

He went through the gate into the park. I waited another ten seconds and then left the car to follow after him. He was a compulsive walker, Mrs. Nichols had said; so he was probably not going anywhere in particular. But the restlessness was still inside me and I was glad to be out and moving around with at least some sense of purpose, to help pass the time.

Talbot led me across the grass to the rim of the grotto, onto a path through the trees, down the steep wooded slope on a series of switchbacked trails. When he reached the grotto he turned to the west, went past and through shaded picnic areas, a wide green with a stage on the south side where concerts were held on summer Sundays, the deserted parking lot that fronted a rustic club building, another green, and finally to the lagoon at the far end.

He stopped on a strip of graveled beach, stood looking out at a handful of ducks floating on the gray water. Rushes and tule grass grew along the near shore; they made me think again of the place at Lake Merced where Christine Webster had been found. The absence of people and the dark sky gave the area a kind of depressingly secluded atmosphere, even though the backsides of several houses on Wawona and Crestlake Drive lined the north and south embankments above. The wind made wet whispery sounds in the pine and eucalyptus branches, built little waves that lapped over the gravel at Talbot's feet.

There were more picnic benches near the lagoon, beneath a shelter-roof attached to a set of restrooms; I started over there just to keep from waiting at a standstill. As I neared the restrooms Talbot turned from the lagoon and plodded up in the same direction, at an angle to the nearest of the benches. But he did not look at me, or even seem to know I was there. He sat on the bench, stiff-postured, as motionless as a block of wood, and stared out at the lagoon again.

I hesitated, debating with myself. There was something about him, a vague impression I could not quite define, that made me want to take a closer look at him. The last thing you want to do on a surveillance is to approach the subject, make him aware of you—but this was not an ordinary surveillance and Talbot was not an ordinary subject. He seemed to have little awareness of externals: a man lost deep inside himself, suffering in his own private hell. If I spoke to him, chances were he would not remember me five seconds afterward.

All right, then. I moved away from the restrooms and circled around to approach him from the front, moving at a casual pace. He did not seem to see me even when I blocked off his view of the lake. I stopped two feet from where he was sitting. His face was narrow and bonily irregular, I saw then, with deep creases like erosion marks in the cheeks and forehead. The whites of his eyes gave the impression of bleeding: his sister had been right about him not sleeping much since the accident. But there was something else in those eyes, in the fixed vacant stare of the pupils—something that made the hair on my neck bristle.

"Excuse me," I said. "Would you have the time?"

It took him three or four seconds to respond; then he blinked slightly and focused on me. "I'm sorry. What did you say?" Polite voice, but as empty as the bloodshot eyes.

"I was just wondering what time it was."

"I'm afraid I don't know. I'm not wearing a watch."

"Thanks anyway." I paused. "Cold out here, isn't it."

"Yes. Cold."

I wanted to talk to him some more but there was nothing else to say. I just nodded and pivoted away, and immediately his gaze fixated on the lagoon again; he had not moved any part of his body except his head during the brief exchange between us.

Back beside the restrooms, I leaned against the wall with my hands shoved deep into the pockets of my coat. The wind seemed colder now. Whether or not Talbot was in danger from Victor Carding, I thought, that look in his eyes said he was in greater danger from himself. Much greater danger.

It was the look of a man who wants to die.

Talbot left the lagoon a little past five, made a perimeter loop of the park on Crestlake Drive and Nineteenth Avenue, and went back into his house. It was dark by then; he put all the lights on one by one, as if he could not bear to face the night hours unless he was surrounded by light. Chasing shadows—literally. But there were no lights to chase the shadows and the darkness that seemed to be inside him.

The minutes between six and eight o'clock dragged away. I stayed in the car the whole time, fidgeting, putting the heater on now and then to keep warm. Once I saw Talbot's silhouette at a window on the Wawona Street side; but it was gone seconds later. He did not come outside again.

Bert Thomas showed up at eight sharp to relieve me. I spent a little time talking to him, letting him know my feelings about Talbot. Then I took myself away from there and drove straight home to my flat.

I had to park three blocks away, which was par for the course; garages are at a premium in Pacific Heights because most of the buildings are older apartment complexes or converted private homes like the one I live in. A ripe smell greeted me when I let myself into the flat; I had forgotten to take out the garbage again. But then, I had never been much of a housekeeper and I was used to ripe smells, dirty dishes, dustballs under the furniture, and soiled laundry and other items scattered around the floors. About the only thing I made an effort to keep neat was my collection of pulps—over six thousand of them now, on standing bookshelves along the living room walls.

In the kitchen I got a beer from the refrigerator. Drank some of it on my way into the bedroom, where I keep the telephone. The bed, as we used to say when I was a kid, looked like it belonged in a whorehouse after a raid; I pushed aside a wad of blankets, sat down on the bare mattress. And lifted the phone receiver and dialed the Nichols' number.

Mrs. Nichols answered. I told her who was calling, and she said immediately, "Is everything all right with Martin? Why aren't you at his house?"

"I've got a man there," I said. "And no, I'm afraid everything isn't all right."

"What? Do you mean Victor Carding—?"

"No, there's been no sign of Carding. It's your brother's mental state I'm worried about, Mrs. Nichols."

"His mental state?"

"I think he might be suicidal," I said.

She made a sound that might have indicated surprise, incredulity, or a combination of both. "That's ridiculous," she said. "Martin? Good God, I told you he was fanatically moral; he'd be the last person in this world to commit suicide. Whatever gave you such an idea?"

"I had a close look at him today. He strikes me as a pretty sick man."

"Nonsense. He'll snap out of it sooner or later. It's just a matter of time."

"I'm not so sure of that, ma'am."

"Well I am."

"Have you tried to get him to see a doctor?"

"I suggested it, yes. For something to help him sleep."

"But he refused?"

"Yes. He has an aversion to drugs."

"Couldn't you talk him into it. Or bring a doctor around to examine him?"

Pause. "My brother is *not* mentally ill," she said in a cold, flat voice. "And I won't have someone like you telling me he is."

Someone like me, I thought. Just another common laborer, and what the hell did common laborers know about anything? I took a swallow of beer to drown the sharp words that were on my tongue; there was nothing to be gained in telling her off.

"Are you still there?"

"Yes. I'm still here."

"You were hired to do a specific job," she said. "I assume you wish to continue doing it. Is that correct?"

I had already asked myself the same question. If I backed off the case she would only hire someone else—assuming she could find someone else to take it on, as unorthodox as it was. Maybe there wasn't much Bert and Milo and I could do to protect Martin Talbot from himself or from somebody else, but at least we could try; at least three people who understood the situation would be keeping a steady watch on him.

And I needed the money. I *needed* that money, damn it.

"Yes," I said.

"Then I'll thank you not to bother me again with your opinions. You're to call only if you have something to report about Victor Carding. And you're to send me a detailed written report at the beginning of next week. Is that understood?"

"Understood."

"Fine. Good-night, then."

"Good night, Mrs. Nichols."

I made the kind of gesture Italians always use to convey disgust and banged down the receiver. Some lady, Laura Nichols. Some nice sister. No mental illness in *her* family, by God. No brother of *hers* could have come unhinged enough to take his own life. Poor Martin was just a little eccentric, that was all. He'd snap out of it eventually; it was only a matter of time.

Poor Martin, all right

Poor bastard.

FIVE

On Thursday morning I spent a couple of hours in my office, going through the mail and catching up on some paperwork. There were no messages on my answering machine and I had no calls while I was there. No one had rung me up at home either, so I assumed that nothing much had happened at Talbot's during the night. Nothing, at least, that Bert or Milo knew about.

I called the Hall of Justice at ten o'clock to check in again with Eberhardt. But he was out on a field investigation, the cop I talked to said, and was not expected back until early afternoon. The cop was not at liberty to say if there were any new developments on the Christine Webster homicide. At eleven-thirty I tried again, just in case; Eb still had not returned. I would just have to wait until tonight, when my shift on Talbot was finished, and then call him at home for an update.

I locked the office, picked up my car, and headed over Twin Peaks to Stern Grove. The weather was better today: still cold and windy, but the overcast had lifted and patches of blue sky were visible between shifting cloud masses. It would make surveillance a little easier because I could spend more time moving around in the park and less time sitting like a lump in the car.

Milo Petrie was waiting for me, standing just inside the park gate, when I came down Wawona off Nineteenth. I made a U-turn alongside the Talbot house, parked where I had yesterday, facing east, and went over to join him.

"How'd it go, Milo?"

"Quiet," he said. He was a lean, hawk-nosed guy in his sixties, bundled up in a heavy car coat, a longshoreman's cap, and a pair of gloves. Like Bert Thomas, he was a retired patrolman out of the Ingleside station. "And goddamn cold, too. I haven't been on an early-morning stakeout in twenty years; almost froze my balls off."

"Anything happen on Bert's shift?"

"He said no. Subject stayed inside and didn't have any visitors. Lights were on all night, like maybe he didn't go to bed."

"Talbot come out this morning?"

"Yep. A little after eight. He walked all the way down Nineteenth to the Stonestown shopping center. Gave me a chance for some exercise, anyway."

"What did he do in Stonestown?"

"Nothing much," Milo said. "Wandered around, sat in the mall for awhile. No contact with anybody. He led me straight back here about thirty minutes ago."

I nodded. "Okay. No need for you to hang around; you look like you could use some coffee and hot food."

"And a stiff shot of brandy." He hesitated, glancing over at the house. "This Talbot's in a pretty bad way, you know? Funny look in his eyes—like he's half-dead inside."

"Yeah, I know."

"I've seen that look before," Milo said. "Jumper on the Golden Gate Bridge had it back in '68; I tried to talk him out of going over but he jumped anyway. You ask me, Talbot's a potential Dutch."

"I've been thinking the same thing. But his sister doesn't believe it, and she's the only one who could have him committed for observation."

"If I was her, I'd be a hell of a lot more worried about him knocking himself off than anyone else trying to do it for him."

"Me too," I said. "But the way things are, I don't see anything we can do except play it her way. And hope for the best."

Milo shook his head. "People," he said.

When he was gone I went through the gate into the park. There were a few more people around today: a couple of kids throwing a football back and forth, a man walking an Irish setter on a leash, an elderly couple carrying a small silver-flocked Christmas tree that they had probably bought at the lot over on Nineteenth and Sloat. I stood on the park road and watched the kids. The one nearest me missed a catch and the ball rolled to a stop about twenty feet away; when he picked it up I called out for him to peg it to me—just being friendly, trying to pass the time. He threw it back to the other kid instead, grinned at me, and gave me the finger.

Christmas trees before Thanksgiving. Citizens letting their dogs crap all over a public recreation area. Young kids giving the finger to adults old enough to be their grandfather. And a twenty-year-old girl lying in the morgue with two bullets in her body. And an honest man, a moral man, tearing himself apart with guilt. And a stubborn, narrow-minded woman who would rather believe in an unlikely threat than in the real danger of mental illness.

People, Milo had said.

Yeah. People.

I walked over to the driving range. Came back to the gate. Walked up the park road again. Watched the kids again, staring at the one who had given me the finger until it made him nervous enough to stop playing catch and head down into the grotto with his friend. The cold was beginning to bother me, as it had yesterday, and I was also a little hungry; I had eaten nothing for breakfast except some cereal. Before leaving my flat, though, I had made some sandwiches, and I had bought a thermos near my office and filled it with coffee. Time for lunch, I thought. I turned back for the gate—

Just in time to see the taxi come gliding along Twenty-first Avenue and pull up in front of the Talbot house.

The driver blew his horn a couple of times. Immediately the front door opened and Martin Talbot appeared, wearing the same tweed overcoat of yesterday. There seemed to be purpose in his stride as he came down the stairs and crossed to enter the cab.

I was running by then, out through the gate and around the front of my car. The taxi pulled away, left on Wawona, as I fumbled the door open and slid inside. If the driver had caught the light at Nineteenth, I might have lost them; midday traffic was pretty heavy along there, clogging all three southbound lanes. But the signal was red, and it stayed red long enough for me to swing out and close to within half a·block.

Talbot's sudden departure by cab was surprising. From what Laura Nichols had told me, he had not gone anywhere since the accident except for those periodic walks around the neighborhood. So why this trip? And why the seeming purpose in his stride?

The taxi swerved over into the left-turn lane at Nineteenth and Sloat; I managed to do the same. And to make the light with them. They cut over onto Junipero Serra, turned left again at Ocean Avenue, and followed Ocean to the City College. Over the hill to Geneva, then, and straight out past the San Mateo County line and the Cow Palace.

An uneasiness had begun to grow in me, and it kept on growing when the driver swung right on Bayshore Boulevard and headed up the long sweeping hill beyond. I was pretty sure I knew where Talbot was going, now. And I was right: on the other side of the hill the cab made another right-hand turn and entered Brisbane on Old Country Road.

My hands were tight around the wheel as I turned in after them. Brisbane was a small town of maybe four thousand people, nestled in the curves and cuts along the eastern slopes of the San Bruno Mountains overlooking the Bay. It had some similarities in appearance and population mix to Sausalito, although it was more of a bedroom community than an artistic one. A place where all sorts of different types lived, from painters and sculptors to business executives to blue collar workers.

It was also the place, Mrs. Nichols had told me, where Victor Carding lived.

Why would Talbot be on his way to see Carding? Three possible answers, as far as I could tell. One—he wanted to talk it out with the man, ask forgiveness, seek some sort of relief for his guilt. Two—he was after punishment instead of relief, either verbal or physical. Three—the initiative was Carding's, not Talbot's, and Talbot was responding to a telephone summons.

The first or the second seemed the most probable. The only reason Carding could have for requesting a meeting was that he intended to carry out his threat; but if you're going to kill a man you don't invite him to your house to do it. The first answer was the best of the lot, though it could still mean trouble; the second was volatile as hell. Dicey situation any way you looked at it.

But the big question was, what was I going to do about it?

I followed the cab up San Bruno Avenue, hanging back a full two blocks. At Glen Parkway it turned right, hooked through the center of town, and then began to climb upward on the network of narrow twisting roads that crisscrossed the slope. Most of the houses up there either clung to the steep hillside below the roads, with carports and entrances at road level, or sat on little knolls or inside man-made cutouts. They ran the spectrum of architectural types and building materials: country cabin, plain frame, box, old Spanish, false Southern Colonial, ultramodern hexagonal and octagonal; brick, redwood, pine, stucco, old gray stone, whitewashed block. The only things they all had in common were balconies and wide picture windows, to take advantage of a panoramic view of the Bay, parts of San Francisco, the East and South Bay cities.

I lost sight of the taxi half a dozen times as we climbed the rutted, switchbacked roads, almost lost it completely once at a three-way intersection. But I was still behind them when they turned onto Queen's Lane, near the highest perimeter of the village. The road looped around and through an undeveloped section—vertical hillside on the left, slope on the right wooded with scrub oak and bay and horse chestnut trees—and the taxi disappeared again for eight or ten seconds. When I neared the center of the loop, where a dirt-faced turnaround had been cut out of the bluff wall, I had them back in sight. And they were just pulling up beyond a gravel driveway seventy-five yards downrange.

I braked, veered over onto the turnaround. Half a minute later Talbot got out of the cab and stood next to a rural-type mailbox, looking up the driveway; from where I was, I could not see the house there. At length he headed up the drive, walking stiff-backed but with that same sense of purpose, and disappeared from sight. The cab stayed where it was, parked on the verge; Talbot had evidently told the driver to wait.

Okay, I thought, here we go. Play it one step at a time. I set the emergency brake, got out, and went down the road at a fast trot. The wind slapped at my face; it was strong up here, pungent with the spicy scent of bay leaves. Overhead the sun seemed to be trying to break through the clouds, creating a bright metallic glare that made me squint.

The house came into view when I was thirty yards from the driveway. It was set on a piece of level ground above the road, its backside close to a notch machine-carved out of the hill—a pretty attractive place for someone Mrs. Nichols had referred to as a "common laborer." Smallish, square-shaped, made out of brick and brick-colored wood. Wide, roofed porch across the front, decorated with planterboxes full of ferns. Half-hidden on the far side was what looked to be a two-car garage; the driveway bent around in that direction.

Talbot was up on the porch, just standing there before the door, waiting.

I slowed to a walk, watching him. Just as I reached the mailbox, he pivoted abruptly and came down off the steps. Nobody home, I thought—but the sense of relief I felt was premature. Talbot stopped after a couple of paces, turned, and stared over toward the garage. A few seconds later he started toward it. And vanished again around the side of the house.

Maybe Carding was at work or had gone somewhere else; but maybe, too, he was out in the garage and had not heard or had chosen to ignore the doorbell. Give Talbot half a minute, I told myself. If he doesn't show by then, better get up there.

Behind me I heard a car door slam. Then a voice yelled, "Hey! You there!"

I turned. It was the cabbie, a youngish guy, heavy-set, wearing a poplin windbreaker and a pugnacious expression. "You talking to me?"

"That's right, buddy. You been following me?"

Ah Christ, I thought, this is all I need.

"Thought I spotted a tail when we started up here," the cabbie said. "What the hell you been following me for?"

"Nobody's following you," I said. I looked up at the house again. Still no sign of Talbot.

"I figure different," the cabbie said belligerently. He came away from the taxi, stopped twenty feet from me, and put his hands on his hips. "I don't stand for shit like that."

The thirty seconds were up. I could feel my chest beginning to tighten; sweat formed cold and sticky under my arms. Something going on in that garage. Talbot would have come out by now if there wasn't.

"You hear what I said, fatso?"

Fatso. I gave him a go-to-hell look and started up the drive, hurrying. The cabbie came after me; I could hear his shoes crunching on the gravel. Wind currents swayed the scrub oak and the brownish grass on the hillside above, made faint whispering murmurs in the afternoon stillness. But nothing moved and nothing made a sound anywhere around the house or the garage.

"Turn around, goddamn it!" the cabbie yelled behind me. "Come on, you son of a bitch!"

That was enough; I could not afford to let it go any further.

I whirled on him, glaring. "I'm here on police business, smart guy," I lied in a hard tight voice. "You understand? Police business. You want to make trouble, fine, I'll have your ass thrown in jail for obstruction of justice."

He pulled up short and blinked at me. Most of the belligerence faded out of his expression; he began to look uncertain and a little worried.

"Now go on, get back to your cab," I said. "And don't say anything about me to your fare when he comes back. *Capici?*"

"Hey," he said, "hey, I'm sorry, man, I didn't know you were a cop—"

"Move it!"

I put my back to him, the hell with him, and trotted the rest of the way up onto the flat. The drive made a wide loop there, around and alongside the house; I cut off it at a sharp angle, onto hard-packed earth. When I neared the porch corner, the whole of the garage materialized ahead of me. One of its double doors was standing part-way open and I could see that there were lights on inside; but that was all I could see. Still no sign of—

And that was when the gun went off.

The flat cracking sound was unmistakable; I had heard the report of a handgun too many times in my life. I broke into a lumbering run. There was no second shot—no other sounds of any kind from inside the garage. Instinct warned me against barging in there, but I did it anyway: I caught the edge of the closed door half and swung myself around it, through the opening by two steps.

I was braced to find a dead man lying on the floor, and that was what I found. But what surprised me, what made me stare wide-eyed, was that it was not Martin Talbot.

The dead man had to be Victor Carding.

He lay sprawled on his side near a long cluttered workbench, both legs bent up toward his chest as if he had tried to assume a fetal position before he died; there was blood all over the front of his blue workshirt. Three feet away, between Carding and a partly open rear window, Talbot stood looking down at the

37

body. His arms were flat against his sides, and in his right hand was a snub-nosed revolver.

The light in there came from a drop-cord arrangement suspended from one of the ceiling rafters; the cord and its grilled bulb cage swayed a little, so that there was an eerie shifting movement of light and shadow across Talbot's face. He looked ghastly: twisted-up expression of sickness and torment, eyes popped and unblinking, mouth slacked open like an idiot's.

The hollow queasy feeling was in my stomach again. And there was a rancid taste in my throat; you can never tell what a man with a gun in his hand will do. But he did not even seem to know I was there. His gaze was half-focused, vacant, and the gun stayed pointed at the floor, loose in his grasp.

I took a couple of cautious steps toward him. He did not move. Three more paces, each one slow and measured, brought me up close on his right. Still no movement. And no resistance when I reached down, closed my hand around the revolver, and eased it out of his cold fingers.

I let out the breath I had been holding and backed off. The gun was a Smith and Wesson .38 caliber; the stubby muzzle was still warm. I dropped it into my coat pocket and sidled around so that the dead man was between Talbot and me. Then I knelt to take a closer look at the body.

No doubt that it was Victor Carding. He matched the description Laura Nichols had given me: thin, gaunt, sallow-faced. He had been shot once in the chest; the blood was coagulating around the wound. There were no other marks on him that I could see, and nothing on the floor near him except a couple of sealed envelopes—PG&E bill, letter from a bank—that might have been jarred out of a pocket when he fell.

When I straightened up Talbot blinked and focused on me for the first time. He said, "I killed him," in a hoarse empty voice—the kind of voice, if you've ever heard it, that can raise the hairs on your scalp.

"Easy, Mr. Talbot."

"He shouted at me, called me a murderer. Because I killed his wife, you see. Murderer, he said. Murderer, murderer."

I went over to him again and took his arm. I wanted him out of there; I wanted out of there myself. The mingled smells of oil and dust, cordite and death, were making me a little nauseous.

"I just . . . I couldn't stand it," Talbot said. "I lost control of myself. The gun . . . it was on the workbench. I picked it up, just to make him stop, but he lunged at me and it went off. I killed him. He was right, I *am* a murderer. . . ."

Gently I prodded him toward the door. He came along without protest, moving like a sleepwalker. Outside, in the wind and the leaden daylight, I took several deep breaths to clear the death-smell out of my nostrils. Both the cabbie and the hack were gone; he had probably heard the shot and decided he wanted no part of what was going on here. Nobody else seemed to have heard it; the nearest neighbor was across the road and fifty yards down.

I took Talbot around the front of the house, up onto the porch. The door was unlocked. Inside, I sat him down in a chair and then hunted up the telephone.

"I murdered him," Talbot said again, as I picked up the receiver. "I murdered him."

No you didn't, I thought. No way.

Talbot had *not* killed Victor Carding.

SIX

It took the local cops exactly fourteen minutes to get there. But it was a long fourteen minutes. Talbot kept staring off into space, dry-washing his hands and muttering over and over the same things he had said in the garage. Watching him and listening to him gave me a creepy, nervous feeling. He was right on the edge of a breakdown—and that was something I was not equipped to handle.

When I finished with my call to the police, I dialed the Nichols' home in Sea Cliff; I figured Laura Nichols ought to know about this as soon as possible. But there was no answer. I put down the receiver and prowled around the living room with Talbot's voice grating in my ears. On the mantelpiece was a framed color photograph of Carding, a plain gray-haired woman, and a kid in his twenties wearing a Fu Manchu mustache. The Carding family—and two of them dead in less than a week. I shook my head and took a turn through the rest of the house, not touching anything. The place was cluttered and dusty, and in the kitchen were a couple of empty bourbon bottles and the smell of spilled whiskey. Aside from that, the condition of each of the rooms seemed ordinary enough.

The distant wail of sirens, when they finally came, was a relief. I went out on the porch to wait and breathe more of the fresh air. The sirens grew louder and closer, and pretty soon a pair of Brisbane police cars came speeding along Queen's Lane, swung up the drive, and plowed to a halt. Three uniformed cops piled out, one of them wearing sergeant's stripes on the sleeve of his jacket. The sergeant's name was Osterman, it turned out, and he was in charge.

I showed him the photostat of my investigator's license, told him about Talbot being inside, answered preliminary questions, and handed over the gun. Osterman told me to wait there; then, before I could explain why I knew Talbot had not shot Victor Carding, he and one of the other cops headed for the garage. The third cop went inside the house to talk to Talbot.

There was a kind of *deja vu* in the next thirty minutes; I had been through it all too often before—the last time just two days ago, at the scene of Christine Webster's murder. More Brisbane police units had arrived and were controlling the inevitable bunch of ghouls that had gathered down on the road. A dark brown Cadillac with MD plates showed up: the doctor I had asked them to send when I called. Then a county ambulance, probably from South San Francisco. Then another car with MD plates, this one containing a harried-looking guy who I assumed was acting coroner for this bailiwick. Then a TV-remote truck that was not permitted up the drive because there was no room; the area in front of the house looked like a parking lot as it was. And while all of this was going on, Osterman went into the house, came back out after ten minutes looking even grimmer than before, and returned to the garage. Neither he nor anyone else said a word to me.

Finally, while I paced back and forth waiting for Osterman to get around to me again, a light-green Ford sedan joined the string of other cars down on Queen's Lane. A fat man in a rumpled suit got out of it, spoke to one of the cops down there, and was allowed to proceed up the drive on foot. The way he moved, in a waddling gait like a latter-day Oliver Hardy, made me stop pacing and stand looking at him as he approached.

Well, what do you know, I thought. Donleavy.

He recognized me at about the same time, raised an eyebrow and then one hand in greeting. I went forward to meet him.

"How are you, Donleavy?"

"Not too bad," he said. We shook hands. "Been what—seven, eight years?"

"About that." I had met him, way back then, during the course of an ugly kidnapping and murder case in Hillsborough—the one on which I had got the knife wound in the belly.

He said, "So what're you doing here? Mixed up with murder again, are you?"

"I'm afraid so. How about you? Aren't you still with the DA's office?"

"Nope. County CID the past four years. Brisbane police don't have the facilities to handle a homicide investigation, so they ask us to come in whenever they get one. I was over in San Bruno on a routine matter; that's why I got sent. Lucky me."

"Lucky you."

"Where's the body?"

"In the garage. The coroner's with it now."

"Any suspects?"

"Yes and no," I said. "There's a man inside the house named Martin Talbot; I found him with the dead man. He had what was probably the death weapon in his hand—a .38 caliber revolver—and he confessed to me that he'd done the shooting. But he didn't do it. I doubt if anybody did; I think it might be suicide."

Donleavy studied me. He looked older, grayer, maybe a little fatter, and his eyes seemed even more sleepy than I remembered them. The impression he gave was one of softness and mildness—but that was an illusion. He was shrewd and dedicated, and he could be pretty tough when he had to be.

42

"You know this Talbot, do you?" he asked.

"I know some things about him. I'm working for his sister."

"Why would he confess to a murder he didn't commit?"

"It's a long story," I said. "You want it now or after you've seen the body and talked to Talbot?"

"Make it after." He clapped me on the arm and waddled off toward the garage.

Another five minutes went away. Then Donleavy returned alone and entered the house. The coroner put in an appearance not long after that, to tell the ambulance attendants that they could have the body. Osterman was with them when they brought it out from the garage; he stood near me, not saying anything, while the attendants loaded the stretcher.

Just as the ambulance started down the drive, the house door opened and everybody inside came out. The local doctor and one of the uniformed cops had Talbot between them, hanging onto his arms; he still moved like a sleepwalker. They put him into the doctor's Cadillac and wasted no time taking him away in the wake of the ambulance.

Donleavy was still up on the front porch; he gestured to me to join him. I did that, with Osterman behind me, and the three of us filed into the living room.

I asked Donleavy, "Did you talk to Talbot?"

"A little. Doctor wanted to get him to the hospital for observation, he's in a pretty bad way."

"He confess to you?"

"Yep, he did."

"To me, too," Osterman said. "It's an open-and-shut case."

"No," I said, "it isn't. He didn't kill Carding."

"What?"

Donleavy said, "Go ahead, you can lay it out now."

"Let me give you the background first." And I told them about the accident in which Carding's wife had been killed. About Talbot's obsessive guilt. About what Laura Nichols had hired me to do. About following Talbot here this afternoon.

"He doesn't sound like a probable murderer, I'll admit that," Donleavy said when I was done. "But he claims he picked up the gun in self-defense, more or less, and it went off by accident. It could have happened that way."

I shook my head. "There are at least three good reasons why it couldn't."

"Which are?"

"One is the time factor," I said. "I was down at the foot of the drive when he disappeared toward the garage. It was thirty seconds before I started up after him, and another two minutes or so until I heard the shot. Say three minutes, maximum. Talbot would have had to walk to the garage, enter, confront Carding, listen to enough verbal abuse to make him pick up the gun, and then shoot Carding when he lunged forward—all in three minutes or less. If that isn't impossible, it's the next thing to it."

"You sure about the amount of time?"

"Positive."

"What's the second reason?"

"Talbot claims Carding shouted at him, shouted accusations. But I didn't hear any shouting; I didn't hear anything at all from the garage until the gun went off. A yelling voice would have carried almost as far as the shot, quiet as it is around here. And I heard the shot loud and clear."

Osterman was frowning. "Maybe Carding didn't shout after all; maybe he spoke in a normal voice and Talbot, mixed up as he is, remembered him as yelling."

"Then why would Talbot have picked up the gun in such a hurry? If somebody's talking to you in a normal or slightly raised voice, even making accusations, you wouldn't have much cause to fear for your safety. Or to grab a weapon just to shut him up."

Donleavy said, "Let's hear the third reason."

"That's the clincher. I took a close look at Carding's body less than five minutes after the shot: the blood around the wound was coagulating. He'd been dead at least fifteen minutes by then, maybe longer."

"You could be wrong about that," Osterman said. "You're not a forensic expert."

"No, but I've seen a lot of blood in my life. Believe me, I can tell the difference between fresh and coagulating."

Donleavy ruminated for a time. Then he said, "Your theory is that Carding killed himself, right?"

"Right. Probably because he was despondent over the death of his wife."

"Gun suicides don't usually shoot themselves in the chest, you know."

"I know. But it happens once in a while—often enough to take it out of the implausible category."

Osterman said, "It doesn't make any sense to me. Why the hell would Talbot shoot off the gun if Carding was already dead? Why would he want to make it look like he'd committed murder?"

"Because he believes he *did* commit murder," I said. "And not just one murder—two. Carding's wife in the accident and now Carding as a result of it."

"Elaborate on that," Donleavy said.

"Look at it this way. Talbot's a man so full of guilt that he can't live with himself; he wants to be punished for what he did—wants to die but doesn't quite have the courage or the strength to take his own life. So he decides to confront Carding, either because he hopes to provoke himself into a suicidal state or because he hopes to provoke Carding into carrying out the threat against his life.

"But when he gets here he finds Carding dead in the garage of a self-inflicted gunshot wound. For Talbot it's a pretty terrible irony: He's the one who wants to be dead, to kill himself, but it's turned out the other way around. He's got a double load of guilt to deal with now and he can't handle it; he really starts to unravel.

"Then he hears the cab driver hassling me out on the drive and realizes somebody's about to find him there with the body. In his mind he's already killed Carding; why not just go ahead and make it look like murder? That way he can be arrested and prosecuted; he won't be dead, but at least he'll be punished.

"He picks up the gun, either from the floor or from Carding's hand, and fires a shot into the roof or one of the walls. And when I come in he blurts out his confession. Simple as that in

45

the factual sense; damned complex in the psychological sense. But I'll bet that's the way it happened."

Osterman was unconvinced. "It still sounds screwy to me," he said.

"Maybe not," Donleavy said. He hooked his fingers around his coat lapels and rocked back and forth; when he did that he looked more than ever like Oliver Hardy. The resemblance was uncanny sometimes, even without the little toothbrush mustache, and it made me wonder if at least some of the mannerisms were calculated—an act to keep the people he dealt with off guard. "I've done some reading in criminal psychology; you should see a few of those case histories."

"Well—if you say so."

"Besides which, there're two empty chambers in the gun and just a single wound in Carding's body. And Talbot only fired one shot."

"Carding could have kept one chamber empty," Osterman said. "Or he could have fired a round days or weeks ago."

"Yeah, I know. Still, you'd better have your men comb the garage for a bullet hole and a .38 slug."

"Whatever you say."

Osterman gave me a curt nod, as if he were annoyed with me for making waves in what he still considered an open-and-shut case and went on out. When he was gone, Donleavy asked me, "What's Laura Nichols' address and telephone number?"

I told him and he wrote the information down in a spiral notebook. "I called her just after I reported the death," I said. "She wasn't home."

"I'll try her again pretty soon," he said. "You got a card for yourself? Home and office numbers?"

"Sure." I handed him one from my wallet.

He said, "I guess that's it for now; you might as well go on home. I'll call you later today or tomorrow."

"Fine."

We shook hands, and I went out and down the wind-swept drive to Queen's Lane. There were still half a dozen citizens hanging around the area; one of them, a kid in his late teens, cut over near me as I turned up toward where I'd left my car.

"What happened up there, mister? Was it a suicide?"

"Yeah. Suicide."

"The old boozehound knocked himself off, huh?" the kid said. "Wow." And he grinned at me.

People.

It was dusk by the time I got back into downtown San Francisco. I went straight to my office and checked the answering machine. No messages. Then I sat down to make some calls.

There was still no answer at the Nichols' home; either Laura Nichols was still out somewhere or she had returned and Donleavy had got in touch with her, and she'd left again to see her brother. I rang up Bert Thomas and Milo Petrie, told each of them the stakeout was finished and what had happened in Brisbane. My last call was to the Hall of Justice, and this time Eberhardt was in. But—

"I'm busy right now," he said. He sounded snippy, the way he does when he's being overworked. "You planning to be home tonight?"

"I was, yeah."

"I'll drop by later, sometime after seven."

I had nothing more to do in the office after that; I locked up again and drove home to my flat. From there I gave the Nichols number another try, with the same nonresults.

I got a beer out of the refrigerator, put a frozen eggplant parmagiana in the oven, and sat down to look at the house mail. The only thing of interest was a sales list from a pulp dealer in Ohio. The guy's prices were kind of high, even for the over-inflated pulp market, but he had three issues of *Thrilling Detective*, one of *Mammoth Mystery,* and one of *FBI Detective* that I needed and that I thought I could afford. I wrote him a letter and a check—and wondered as I did so just how much I had spent this year on pulps. Too much, probably; that was one of the reasons why I was always short of money. But then, outside of my work, collecting pulps was the only real passion I had in life. What good was money if not to use to indulge your passions?

The telephone rang while I was eating my supper. A reporter from the *Chronicle* wanting to know if I had any statement to make concerning the murder of Victor Carding. I said no, politely, and hung up. When I had finished supper and was putting the dirty dishes into the sink with the other dirty dishes the phone rang a second time. Another reporter, this one from one of the TV stations. I told him the party he was looking for had been called to Los Angeles on business and would not be back for a week. Who was I? An associate named Phil Marlowe, I said, and then hung up on him too. Media people bring out the worst in me—I suppose because their business is disseminating sensationalistic crime news and mine relies on avoiding too much lurid publicity. The public eye versus the private eye.

I tried once more to call Laura Nichols. Nobody picked up this time, either. So I plunked myself down in the living room with a 1936 issue of *Popular Detective,* to read and wait for Eberhardt.

The phone rang again at seven fifteen. Another damned reporter? I went into the bedroom and caught up the receiver and said hello with my finger on the cut-off button.

But it wasn't a reporter. "This is Donleavy," his soft sleepy voice said in my ear. "I've got some news for you."

I took my finger off the button. "Good news, I hope."

"Not from your point of view. I talked to Talbot again; so did a couple of psychologists. He still maintains he's guilty and nobody can shake him. We've got no choice except to charge him with suspicion of homicide."

"What? Christ, I explained why he couldn't have done it."

"Sure you did. But you *could* be wrong about the time element and the silence in the garage before the shot. And about the blood coagulation, too; coroner wasn't able to pinpoint the exact time of death. I'm not saying you are wrong, understand. Just that the rest of the evidence indicates you might be."

"What evidence? Look, didn't Osterman's men find a second bullet in the garage?"

"No," Donleavy said, "they didn't."

"But it's got to be there. Otherwise the whole thing doesn't make sense."

"It makes sense the way Talbot tells it."

"No, it doesn't. There's just no way he could have killed Carding. The man committed suicide."

Donleavy made an audible sighing sound. "You're a hundred percent wrong about that, my friend," he said. "Lab boys tested the victim's hands for nitrate traces and his clothing for powder marks; there weren't any. He hadn't fired a gun and he wasn't shot at point blank range: it couldn't possibly be suicide. Victor Carding *was* murdered."

SEVEN

When Donleavy rang off I went into the kitchen, got out another bottle of beer, and sat brooding with it at the table. I had been so positive I was right about the day's events in Brisbane—and I still thought so, damn it, at least where Martin Talbot's actions and motivations were concerned. No way could I have been mistaken about the time element *and* the silence before the shot *and* the coagulating blood; I had been sharply conscious of time, I had been listening for sounds of any kind, I knew well enough when blood was coagulating and when it was fresh. So it added up the same way as before: Talbot had found Carding dead, picked up the gun, and fired a harmless shot—because he believed, just as I had believed, that Carding committed suicide, and because of a double-dose of guilt and a desire for punishment.

But then where the hell was the second bullet? It had to be in the garage; why hadn't Osterman's men found it?

The real surprise, though, was the fact that Carding was not a suicide but a murder victim. A man whose wife has just died in an automobile accident seems an unlikely candidate for homicide; you would think that old enemies, for instance, would consider the tragic loss of a loved one retribution enough. It could have been one of those random thrill killings—but that kind of psychopathic personality usually ties up his victims or slays them execution-style, and in addition almost never leaves his weapon behind. It could have been a burglar whom Carding surprised in the act—but as messy as the house was, it had not been searched for valuables; and burglars, like psychotics, seldom leave weapons behind. Anyway, what would a burglar be doing in the garage in the first place? It could have been a drinking companion of Carding's, and the shooting a result of a drunken argument—but the body had not smelled of alcohol when I examined it, nor were there any whiskey bottles that I could remember seeing in the garage. So again, why would Carding have been shot there instead of inside the house?

Speculation was not going to get me anywhere, I decided. There were just too many things I did not know. About Victor Carding: What kind of man had he been? What kind of life had he led, who were his friends and his enemies? And also about the gun: Did it belong to Carding? If not, was it registered to anyone else? Or traceable in any other way?

Maybe the answers to one or more of those questions would point up the truth. Or maybe Donleavy and Osterman would get lucky and find a neighbor who had seen the killer leave and could identify him. Talbot and the cabbie and I would have seen him ourselves if we had arrived just a short time earlier; Carding could not have been dead more than a few minutes when I found him.

Well, in any case Donleavy was a first-rate cop and it was a good bet that he would get to the bottom of things sooner or later. Which was enough for me—but what about Laura Nichols? How was she taking it? Assuming she knew by now: I had neglected to ask Donleavy, in the wake of his revelations, if he had got in touch with her.

I stood and returned to the bedroom and redialed the Nichols number. This time, on the fourth ring, there was an answering click; Karen Nichols' voice said a moment later, "Yes? Hello?"

"Is your mother there, Karen?" I asked when I had identified myself.

"No. She left hours ago."

"Do you know what happened today?"

"Yes. Some friends and I were at Civic Center all afternoon; I just found out a few minutes ago. Mother left me a note to call her at the hospital. God, it's just terrible. I still can't believe it."

"Your uncle didn't kill Victor Carding," I said.

"I know that. He couldn't hurt anyone. But the police think he did, in spite of what mother says you told them. They have him under arrest at the hospital."

"They'll change their minds when they've had a chance to investigate further."

"Are you really sure of that?"

"Pretty sure. Did your mother say when she'll be home? I'd like to talk to her."

"No, she didn't. But she wants to talk to you, too. She said to give you a message if you called: You're to see her tomorrow morning as early as possible."

"At your home?"

"Yes."

"Did she tell you why, specifically?"

"Mother never tells me why she does anything," Karen said, and there was undisguised bitterness in her voice. "Never. She just goes ahead and does it."

I let a couple of seconds pass before I said, "I'll come by around nine, then."

"All right."

"And try not to worry. Your uncle's receiving the medical care he needs; things'll work out okay in the long run."

"Will they? I hope you're right."

We said goodbye and I put the receiver back into its cradle. I hoped I was right too—and I also hoped that Mrs. Nichols did not want to see me tomorrow morning so she could tell me face to face what a lousy detective she thought I was. She was not the most understanding and compassionate of women; the way she treated and alienated her daughter was proof of that. So she was probably capable of blaming me for not keeping her brother—and the family name—out of this mess; and of stopping payment on the retainer check she'd given me. Which would make a difficult situation even more difficult.

But then, maybe she had something else on her mind. Unpredictable was another adjective you could use to describe her.

In the living room I sat down again with the issue of *Popular Detective* and tried to read. No good; I was too restless now to concentrate on the exploits of pulp detectives. I put the magazine aside and wondered when Eberhardt was going to show up.

Two seconds later, in the crazy coincidental way things happen sometimes, the downstairs door buzzer went off. I crossed to the speaker unit mounted beside the door, pushed the Talk button, and asked who it was. Sure enough, Eberhardt's voice said, "It's me, hot shot. Buzz me in."

I buzzed him in. And then opened the door and waited for him to come clomping up the stairs and along the hall. When he reached me he nodded and grunted something unintelligible. Moved past me to stand looking around at my sloppy housekeeping, his head wagging in a mildy disgusted way, as I shut the door.

"You ever clean up this pigsty?"

"Only when I'm entertaining a lady."

"Not getting much, then, are you?"

"Not getting much," I agreed. "Sit down. You want some coffee? A beer?"

"Make it a beer."

I went to the kitchen, got a couple of bottles of Schlitz out of the refrigerator. When I came back Eberhardt had cleared some of the crap off the sofa and was sitting with his legs splayed

53

out in front of him. He looked tired, irritable, and even more sour-faced than usual.

He said as I handed him a beer, "Seems you had a pretty busy day for yourself."

"You heard about what happened in Brisbane?"

"I heard about it, all right. Makes two murders in two days you're mixed up in."

"Eb, I'm not mixed up in the Christine Webster shooting."

"No, huh?" he said mildly.

"No." I sat down. "Any leads yet on who killed her?"

"Nothing definite. We haven't been able to trace her movements past seven P.M. on Tuesday. Her roommate, Lainey Madden, had a date that night; and just before she left at seven, Christine told her she was planning to spend a quiet evening at home."

"How about a lead on why she had my card in her purse?"

"That we've got," Eberhardt said.

"You do? What is it?"

"She'd been getting anonymous letters and telephone calls," he said. "The threatening kind. Lainey Madden says she was considering going to a private detective about them."

"Were they death threats?"

"Not in so many words. Veiled stuff."

"How long had she been getting them?"

"About two weeks."

"She have any idea who was responsible? Or why?"

"Not according to the Madden girl. Neither of them could imagine why anyone would have it in for Christine."

"Could it be a sex thing?"

"Maybe yes, maybe no." Eberhardt took some of his beer. "Christine kept the letters and the roommate turned them over to us; nothing sexual or obscene in any of them. Or in any of the calls either, apparently. There *is* a sex angle, though. Which you already know about if you read today's papers."

"I didn't read them; I guess I should have. What is it?"

"She was pregnant," he said.

"Ah—Jesus."

"Yeah. Four months along."

"You get a line on the father?"

"Damned good line. She was engaged to a kid she met at S.F. State last semester. Only man in her life the past six months, Lainey Madden says."

"What did the kid have to say when you talked to him?"

"We didn't talk to him. He's disappeared."

"Disappeared?"

"Missing since last Sunday night. From up at Bodega Bay."

Bodega Bay was on the coast about sixty-five miles north of San Francisco. I asked, "What was he doing up there?"

"Working in the commercial fishing business," Eberhardt said. "He decided to skip school this semester, the way we heard it, because he was running low on money. Nobody's seen or heard from him since around nine P.M. on Sunday."

"Well, I guess that makes him your number one suspect."

"Sure. But it's not as simple as it might look. Not by a damn sight, it isn't."

"You mean because of the threats? Maybe the kid made them himself."

"Maybe. Thing is, there're complications now—a whole new can of worms."

"What can of worms?"

"One you seem to be smack in the middle of."

"Me?"

"You. And the missing kid."

"Eb, what the hell are you getting at?"

"The kid's name is Jerry Carding," Eberhardt said sourly. "He's Victor Carding's son."

EIGHT

I sat there and gawked at him. All I could think of to say was, "Jesus Christ."

"Uh-huh," he said.

"When did you find this out?"

"Yesterday afternoon. Didn't mean much then, where you're concerned; I didn't know you were working on a case that involved Victor Carding. Logan and Klein went to Brisbane to talk to Carding last night. That's how we learned the kid is missing; Carding's been trying to locate him ever since the accident, to tell him about his mother's death. He didn't have any idea where Jerry might have disappeared to, he said. Told the inspectors his son was in love with Christine, couldn't possibly have killed her—the usual stuff you expect to hear from a father. And that was it, until we heard about his murder late this afternoon and how you were involved in that too."

I stood up and took a couple of turns around the room; I was still trying to get my thoughts sorted out. Eberhardt drank beer and watched me expressionlessly.

After a time he said, "I talked to your friend Donleavy before I came over here; he filled me in. He also told me the nitrate test on Carding's hands proved negative, and that there weren't any powder marks on his clothing. So it couldn't have been suicide the way you thought."

"I know. He called me with the same news."

"How sure are you this Martin Talbot is innocent?"

"Positive. I'd swear to it in court."

"It'd make things simpler if you were wrong."

"I suppose so." I lowered myself into the chair again. "First Christine Webster, then Victor Carding. And Jerry Carding is missing. You think he could have been a target too?"

"You mean murdered like the others? Some nut with a grudge wasting not only what's left of the Carding family but also the kid's girlfriend? Come on."

"Hell, crazier things have happened," I said. "It *could* be a psycho deal."

"I doubt it. Not that kind."

"So maybe not. But there's another kind I can think of."

"I'll bet I know what it is. The kid himself is a psycho; he went berserk and murdered both his girl and his old man. Right?"

"Right. That would pretty much explain everything, including his disappearance."

"Sure it would," Eberhardt said. "It's the best theory we've got so far. But it's also got too many holes and loose ends to suit me."

"Such as?"

"The kid's character profile, for one thing. Friendly, serious-minded, well-adjusted; wants to be a journalist. No quirks, no apparent hangups. Pacifist on political and ideological issues. Everybody Logan and Klein talked to said he's got strong feelings against violence of any kind."

"People aren't always what they seem to be, Eb. Things can

happen inside them—pressures, compulsions, psychological shifts."

"You think I don't know that? But there are usually indications, small attitude changes of one kind or another. And according to the people who know him, Jerry Carding's the same kid he always was.

"Then why did he vanish all of a sudden?"

"Yeah—why? I sent a man up to Bodega Bay today, but he hasn't been able to dig up any answers so far." Eberhardt got out a pipe and a pouch of tobacco, began loading one from the other. "Anyhow," he said then, "another thing is the time element. The kid dropped out of sight on Sunday, Christine was killed on Tuesday, and Victor Carding was murdered today. If somebody goes berserk, it doesn't take him two days to commit his first homicide and two more days to commit his second."

He was right, of course. But for the sake of argument I said, "So maybe he didn't go berserk. Maybe he just went insane—the cunning kind of psychosis. He plans his murders, carries them out at two-day intervals."

"Nuts," Eberhardt said. "And that's not a pun. Cunning lunatics don't go after friends and members of their own families; they pick random victims. They also operate in a set pattern, the same kind of MO in each case. There's no pattern here. Take the weapons, for instance."

"Weapons? Plural?"

"Plural. Webster and Carding weren't shot with the same gun. The girl was killed with a .32 caliber weapon—and there was no sign of it near her body. Carding was killed with the .38 you found in Talbot's hand. Like I said: no pattern, but plenty of holes and loose ends."

"You figure two different murderers, then?"

"Not necessarily. But it looks that way."

I did a little brooding. "Has Donleavy been able to trace the .38?"

"No. It doesn't seem to be registered anywhere. Probably an outlaw weapon."

"But it could have belonged to Victor Carding."

"It could have."

"And so could the missing .32."

"I suppose so."

"Was Carding upset about Christine's death?"

"Klein said he was, yeah."

"What did he have to say about his son's relationship with her?"

"Not much. Why?"

"Did he seem to approve of it?"

"Yes. What are you leading up to?"

"A possible answer, maybe."

"Which is?"

"Suppose Carding hated Christine for some reason," I said. "Suppose he was responsible for those threatening calls and letters. And suppose he was the one who killed her—lured her out to Lake Merced on some sort of pretext; she knew him well enough to have gone there to meet him after dark. Then suppose Jerry found out about it, confronted his father today, lost his head and grabbed up the .38 and shot him. Revenge motive."

Eberhardt lit his pipe. "I don't like it much," he said between draws.

Neither did I, but I said, "It is possible."

"Possible, but damned unlikely. Donleavy and the Brisbane police searched the Carding property; they'd have found the .32 if it was there."

"Carding could have got rid of it after shooting the girl."

"Okay, I'll give you that point. But what's the motive? Why would a man hate his son's girlfriend enough to want her dead?"

"I don't know. Maybe he was the unbalanced one, not Jerry. Maybe his wife dying sent him around the bend."

"He'd still need a motive, crazy or not."

"Well, what kind of guy was he? What were his attitudes, prejudices, things like that?"

"We're still checking and so is Donleavy. But he seems to've been a pretty average sort. Worked as a carpenter and construction laborer, built the Brisbane house himself fifteen years ago, got along well with his neighbors. Devoted to his wife and had a good relationship with Jerry, who's an only child; Klein says he was grieving deeply over the wife's death and worried about the kid's disappearance. His only vice appears to've been booze. He'd been arrested once for drunk driving and once for public drunkenness, and he was about half-smashed last night—a borderline alcoholic." Eberhardt shrugged and wreathed himself in a cloud of pipe smoke. "There's nothing in any of that to support your theory."

"No," I said.

"It just won't wash. It doesn't explain why Jerry disappeared from Bodega Bay, or why he wouldn't have surfaced between Sunday and today. And how could he have known his old man was the one who killed Christine? Clairvoyance?"

"Okay, Eb, it was just an idea."

"You got any others you want to hash out?"

"No. I don't suppose the neighbors noticed anything today, before Talbot and I showed up?"

"Uh-uh. Donleavy and the Brisbane cops drew a blank."

I finished my beer, thought about getting another one, and decided against it; my stomach already felt bloated and gaseous. For a time I watched Eberhardt pollute the room with more acrid pipe smoke. It had a heavy smell and it made my nostrils itch. Give me cigarette smoke any day, I thought—good old cigarette smoke. Finally I stood and went over and opened one of the bay windows a little, to let in some fresh cold air.

"Still bothers you, huh?" Eberhardt said when I came back.

"What?"

"Not being able to smoke yourself."

"Sometimes. Not too much anymore."

"You're a hell of a lot better off. I wish I could quit."

"You could if you had something growing on a lung."

He made a face. "Yeah," he said.

I stifled a belch and sat down again. "You think it's possible that the two murders are unrelated?"

"Anything's possible."

"But you don't think so."

"Hell no. Jerry Carding's girlfriend and father both get shot to death within two days of each other, and the kid himself drops out of sight; there's got to be a connection somewhere." He paused and tapped the stem of his pipe against his teeth. "There's already one connection we know about," he said.

"Meaning me."

"Right. Your business card is in the girl's purse; you're working for the sister of the guy who accidentally killed Carding's wife; and you find Carding's body."

"That *is* coincidence, Eb. At least as far as I know."

"Maybe. Maybe not. First you heard of Victor Carding and the Talbot/Nichols clan was yesterday morning?"

I nodded. "After I left you at Lake Merced."

"Any special reason why the Nichols woman picked you out of all the other private eyes in the book?"

"She didn't tell me if there was."

"What did she have to say about Carding?"

"Just that he'd threatened her brother's life after the accident, and tried to attack him, and she was afraid he might come after Talbot again."

"She didn't indicate she knew Carding personally?"

"No. She called him a 'common laborer,' but that doesn't have to mean anything."

"Did she mention Jerry Carding at all?"

"No."

"Well, that corroborates what she told Klein and Logan tonight. They talked to her at the hospital where Talbot's being held. She says she never laid eyes on either of the Cardings or heard of them before the accident. Talbot claimed the same thing a little while later."

"What about Karen Nichols?"

"Who's she?"

"Mrs. Nichols' daughter. She's a few years older than Jerry and Christine, but they're still in the same general age group. It could be she knew one or both, or at least knew of them."

"I'll have Klein talk to her tomorrow. Anybody else in the immediate family?"

"Not that I know about. I got the impression Laura Nichols is either a widow or divorced."

Eberhardt smoked in silence for a time. Then he said, "This job Mrs. Nichols hired you to do—didn't it strike you as a little screwy?"

"Sure. But she was determined, and I couldn't see any reason for turning her down."

"Let's try this on for size: She had an ulterior motive in setting up a round-the-clock surveillance on her brother."

"Like what?"

"Like she wanted to provide him with an alibi. If he was being watched at all times by a team of private detectives, he couldn't be suspected of Carding's murder. Only Talbot crossed her up by deciding to pay a call on Carding today."

"Which would make her Carding's killer?"

"Right. And the motive could be that she was more afraid of Carding carrying out his threat against Talbot then she let on; so she decided to take care of Carding before he had a chance to come after her brother."

"I don't know, Eb," I said. "I guess she could be loony enough to come up with a plot like that, but it sounds farfetched to me. TV cop show stuff."

"Yeah, you're right. I don't buy it either. It doesn't involve a connection with Christine Webster, or explain the kid's disappearance or half a dozen other things."

We kicked it around a while longer, over another beer each, but we were both fresh out of workable theories. The problem was, there still weren't enough facts in yet—and the pieces we did have were jumbled and shaped with odd angles. It might be days or weeks before the right pattern began to emerge. If it ever emerged at all.

Eberhardt left at eleven-thirty and I went straight to bed. But my mind was too full of questions to shut down right away; I tossed around for more than an hour before I finally drifted off. The whole business was damned frustrating. I was involved and yet I was not involved. I was a link between the two murders and yet I knew little about any of the people or any of the motivations and relationships in either case. The idea of sitting passively by waiting to be told bits and pieces as they developed did not appeal to me much—and yet there was nothing else I could do.

What could I do?

NINE

The weather shifted again on Friday morning, the way it often does from day to day in San Francisco: A thick fog had come rolling in and turned the city into a bleak study in gray. It was particularly heavy in Sea Cliff, obliterating most of the ocean and Bay and all of the Golden Gate Bridge when I got out there a few minutes past nine. Most of the time I like the fog—it can create a certain sinister atmosphere, or the illusion of it, that appeals to my imagination. But not on this day; it seemed more depressing than anything else and made me feel as gray as everything looked.

I left my car in front of the Nichols house and plodded up the terraced steps and pushed the doorbell button. Pretty soon the peephole opened; the eye that peered out at me this time belonged to Laura Nichols. The peephole closed again and the door swung inward.

She was wearing a lavender pants suit today, but she did not look quite as poised or self-assured; the blonde hair was less carefully coiffed and there were dark smudges under the amber eyes. When she said, "Come in, please," her voice seemed subdued, with none of the coldness or arrogance of Wednesday night. So maybe she isn't going to give me any trouble, I thought. Which would be a good thing for both of us; the way I felt I was just liable to backtalk her if she started in on me.

I entered, gave her my coat, and then followed her down the tiled hallway. The living room seemed even darker and more cheerless today because of the fog swirling on the patio beyond the glass doors. I sat on the sofa again and she sat on the same chair as before, and we looked at each other.

She said, "Thank you for coming."

"Sure. I'm sorry about your brother, Mrs. Nichols."

"Yes. So am I, God knows."

"How is he?"

"Not good." She played with the diamond ring on her finger, took a breath as if preparing herself for a difficult chore, and looked back at me. "I . . . well, I owe you an apology. It seems you were quite right about Martin's mental state."

I did not say anything.

"I should have listened to you," she said. "But it seemed so . . . I just couldn't believe . . ."

She broke off and glanced away; emotions flickered across her face. She was under a good deal of strain, it seemed—and it was not easy for a woman like her to admit to a serious mistake in judgment. But at least she *was* admitting it, which was a point in her favor. And to a virtual stranger at that. I felt myself softening toward her. Not much, but a little.

I asked, "What do the doctors say?"

"That Martin has suffered a severe guilt trauma followed by suicidal depression."

"Will they be able to bring him out of it?"

"They have no opinion yet," she said. "What they're afraid of is that he's lost all will to live and may never regain it."

"Do they believe his confession?"

"They say they can't be sure. Martin keeps insisting he murdered Victor Carding; he seems to believe it even if it isn't true."

"Has he been charged yet?"

"Yes. The county policeman, Donleavy, claims they had no choice." She appealed to me with her eyes. "You told them he couldn't have done it. Why wouldn't they believe you?"

"They don't disbelieve me," I said. "But it's your brother's word against mine, and all the evidence seems to agree with his version of what happened."

"Damn the evidence!" she said with sudden vehemence. "That's all I've heard since last night—from the police, from my attorney, and now from you. Martin is *innocent*."

"Yes, ma'am. And the chances are good the police will prove that themselves, even if your brother won't retract his confession. They're not going to stop investigating; sooner or later they'll dig up the truth."

"Will they? And if they don't?"

"I can't answer that, Mrs. Nichols," I said. "I don't think he'll be brought to trial; but if he is, my testimony might be enough to convince a jury—"

"Martin must *not* be brought to trial," she said. "I couldn't bear the ordeal, the publicity . . . no, it has to be resolved now, as soon as possible."

My feelings toward her quit softening and went the other way again. The ordeal, the publicity—yeah. She was suffering, all right, but it was as much for herself as it was for Martin Talbot. Bad enough that he was mentally ill and had been charged with homicide; what if he was put on public display in a courtroom and then convicted? What would her friends and neighbors say? How could she hold her head up?

"I want you to conduct your own investigation," she said.

That caught me off guard; I was still thinking what a cold and self-pitying woman she was. I blinked at her. "Me?"

"Yes. I have confidence in your ability and your methods. If anyone can get to the bottom of this quickly, you can."

Sure I can, I thought. I said, "I doubt that, Mrs. Nichols.

There's nothing much I could do that the police aren't already doing themselves."

"The police think Martin is guilty; they won't be trying to prove his innocence. You will be because you *know* he's innocent."

"I'm not sure they'd allow me to work on a murder case, even on a peripheral basis," I said. "They don't like private citizens getting involved."

"You won't be interfering with them, will you? Why should they prevent you from earning your living? Besides, aren't you already involved?"

I hesitated. She was right, of course, and not just about my being already involved. I had got permission in the past to make private inquiries on cases involving homicide, so long as I did not get in the way and promised to report any findings immediately. I doubted that Eberhardt would turn me down on this one; he might even feel my poking around was a good idea, considering the circumstances. And the same went for Donleavy, too.

What could I do? I had asked myself last night. Well, this was the answer. If I undertook an investigation it would give me a chance to help Talbot if I could—for his sake, not for Laura Nichols'—and a chance to do something about the death of Christine Webster. It would also keep me active, and keep me involved so maybe I could find out for myself why I *was* involved.

And then there was the money . . . .

"All right," I said, "I'll do what I can, Mrs. Nichols. But on two conditions."

"Yes?"

"One, that the police allow it. And two, that you're completely honest with me."

She bristled a little at that. "Do you suppose I haven't been honest with you?"

"I didn't say that. I only meant that I can't do anything at all for your brother unless I know everything you know. Is there anything you didn't tell me the other day? About him, or about the accident, or about Victor Carding?"

"Of course not. I kept nothing back."

"You'd never heard of Carding before the accident?"

"I had not."

"What about his son Jerry?"

"I didn't know he had a son until the police told me at the hospital last night."

"Christine Webster?"

"No."

"Lainey Madden?"

"No. Who is she?"

"The dead girl's roommate."

"I'm not familiar with the name."

"Was anybody else involved in the accident?"

"No. Only Martin and the Cardings.

"Did Carding make any other threats against your brother? Call him at home later, write him a letter?"

"I'm sure he didn't. Martin would have told me."

I had been watching her pretty closely; if any of her answers had been lies or evasions, I could not tell it from her expression or from her voice. "Just one more question," I said. "How did you happen to pick me when you decided to hire a detective?"

"You were recommended to me."

"By whom?"

"My attorney, Arthur Brown. I asked him for the name of a competent investigator and he gave me yours. He said you had once done some work for another of his clients."

The name was familiar; I remembered meeting Brown once a couple of years ago, through the client she'd mentioned—a civil case involving a substantial damage suit. He was a partner in an old, established Sutter Street law firm and had, as far as I knew, an impeccable reputation.

So much for that. I got up on my feet; I was more than ready to be on my way—not just because I was anxious to go to work, but also because I wanted out of that dark cheerless house and out of Laura Nichols' company. Working for her was one thing. But the less I had to do with her otherwise, the better I would feel.

We said a few more things to each other, about my calling her right away if I had any trouble with the police, about money, about verbal and written reports. Then she showed me to the door. Neither of us bothered to say goodbye.

I drove through the fog to Geary Boulevard, stopped at a service station there, and called the Hall of Justice from their pay phone. Eberhardt was in his office—and in a foul mood, too. When he came on the wire he said irascibly, "You going to check in ten times a day, maybe? There's nothing new; I just got off the phone with Donleavy."

"I didn't call to check in," I said. I told him about the interview with Mrs. Nichols and her proposal that I conduct a private investigation.

"I might have figured," Eberhardt said. "You don't know when to quit, do you?"

"I guess not. Is it okay if I go ahead?"

"Hell, I don't care. You know the rules."

"You mind if I talk to Lainey Madden?"

"Be my guest."

"Could you let me have the address?"

"What am I, your flunky? Look it up in the goddamn phone book. She's listed."

And he banged the receiver down in my ear.

TEN

Edgewood Avenue, off Parnassus near the University of California Medical Center, was a hillside street so steep you had to park perpendicular to the curb. I squeezed my car into a slot a third of the way up, directly in front of the address I had found in the telephone book. The building was an old Eastlake Victorian that had long ago been cut up into apartments; but its facade had undergone a recent facelift and its gables and columns and porch pediments were painted in bright colors—orange and blue, mostly—like a lot of refurbished Victorians in the city these days.

I went up past a couple of Japanese elms to the front porch. On the row of four mailboxes there I found *C. Webster—L. Madden* listed for Number Three; I pushed the intercom button above the box. There was no response at first and I thought that maybe she was not home after all; when I'd dialed her number from the pay phone I had gotten a busy signal and taken that to mean she was in. But then the speaker unit made a staticky noise and a woman's voice said, "Yes? Who is it?"

I told her who it was and why I was there. Silence for a few seconds; then the voice asked, "You're the detective the police told me about? The one whose card Chris had?"

"Yes, that's right."

The electronic lock on the door began to buzz. I got over there and inside and climbed an old-fashioned staircase to the second floor. The door with the numeral three on it was closed; but as soon as I knocked it edged partway open on a chain. Half of a pale face appeared in the opening.

"May I see some identification?"

"Sure." I got my wallet out and held the photostat of my license up for her to look at.

When she finished examining it she closed the door long enough to take the chain off and then pulled it wide. She was a pretty girl about Christine's age, with long straight black hair and huge sad colt-brown eyes; the pale skin had a translucent quality, etched now with lines and shadows. She was wearing what may or may not have been mourning clothes: black slacks and a black pullover sweater.

"I'm sorry if I seemed suspicious," she said. "It's just that what happened to Chris has made me a little paranoid."

"I understand," I said.

She stood aside and let me come in. The living room was good-sized, furnished with inexpensive items made of blonde wood and upholstered in bright patterns, decorated in a way that was feminine without being girlish. Impressionistic oil paintings hung on three of the walls, and there were a lot of colored glass mobiles suspended from the ceiling. On one end table was an enormous white paper rose in a pewter vase.

Lainey sat on the couch, drawing her knees up under her; I took one of the chairs. "I know this must be a difficult time for you," I said tentatively. "I won't keep you long."

"It's all right. I want to do everything I can. Are you working with the police?"

"No. For Martin Talbot's sister."

"Oh—yes. I read about Jerry's father in the papers this morning; it was a shock all over again. It's all so . . . frightening."

I had no words for that; I just nodded.

"Poor Jerry," she said. "First Chris being killed and then his father. . . ." She shivered and was silent.

"Do you know Jerry well?" I asked.

"Pretty well. I met him when Chris started going with him about six months ago."

"How did they meet?"

"A friend of Jerry's introduced them at State."

"Could you tell me the friend's name?"

"Dave Brodnax."

"How would I get in touch with him, do you know?"

"Well, I don't know where he lives, but he's still going to State. And he's on the football team."

"What about Jerry's other friends? Do you know any of them?"

"The only one I've met is Steve Farmer," Lainey said. "He used to go to State too, but he's been working in Bodega Bay for almost a year. He's the one who got Jerry his job up there."

"When did you last see Jerry?"

"Two weeks ago. He came down on the weekend to see Chris."

"Did he usually come down on weekends to see her?"

"Yes. Except for this past one."

"Why didn't he come then?"

"He told Chris he had some important work to do."

"Did he say what it was?"

"No. Just that it was something he was writing."

"Writing? You mean creatively?"

"I guess so. He wants to be a journalist; maybe it was an article or something. He did one once on salmon fishing and sold it to the *Examiner* for their Sunday magazine."

"Did he give any indication that he might be planning to leave Bodega Bay on Sunday night?"

"Chris didn't tell me if he did."

"And you don't have any idea why he disappeared or where he might have gone?"

"No, none. That's part of what makes everything so confusing—Jerry disappearing like that, for no reason. . . ."

I asked, "Did Jerry know Christine was going to have a baby?"

It was five or six seconds before she answered that. Wetness glistened in her eyes, as if she were thinking of the death not only of her friend but of Christine's unborn child; she swallowed a couple of times. "Yes," she said. "Chris told both of us when Jerry was here that last time."

"While all three of you were together?"

"No, separately. But I know she told him because she said so."

"What was his reaction?"

"Well, neither of them wanted to have a baby right away. But Chris wanted it and so did Jerry. They weren't going to, you know, have an abortion."

This line of questioning was not getting me anywhere. And it was making me feel awkward and uncomfortable because of the tears it had put in Lainey's eyes. I went on to something else.

"Did you know Jerry's father?"

"No, I never met him."

"Had Christine met him?"

"Yes. A couple of times."

"Did they get along?"

"I think so. Chris said he drank a lot, but she seemed to like him anyway."

"Did Jerry ever talk about him?"

"Talk about him?"

"What kind of relationship they had, like that?"

"Not that I can remember," Lainey said. A pair of angular creases like an inverted V formed above the bridge of her nose. "Do you think there's some sort of connection between Chris' murder and Mr. Carding's? Is that why you're asking about him?"

"It's possible, yes."

"But I thought Martin Talbot killed Jerry's father. I mean, the papers said he confessed. . . ."

"He did confess," I said, "but he wasn't telling the truth. He's a sick man. But he's not a murderer."

The frown creases deepened. "You can't believe *Jerry* did it? Not just to Chris but his own father? That's crazy. He'd have to be some kind of monster and he's not, he's just not."

"I don't believe it," I said. Which was not the whole truth—I didn't disbelieve it yet, either—but it was what she wanted to hear. "Still, it's a fact that both his fiancee and his father were murdered within two days of each other. And that he's disappeared."

She shook her head in a numb way and hugged herself, as though she felt chilled.

I asked gently, "Had you ever heard of Martin Talbot before you read his name in the papers this morning?"

"No. Never."

"Do the names Laura Nichols or Karen Nichols mean anything to you?"

"Nichols? No, nothing." Another headshake. "I just can't understand any of this. It seemed so obvious who'd killed Chris, and now . . . "

"Obvious who'd killed her?"

"Yes. She'd been getting threatening calls and letters for more than two weeks. Did you know about that?"

I nodded.

"Well, I thought it was him, the motherfucker."

The last word made me blink. I had more or less grown used to hearing women young and old use street language, the way a lot of them did these days, but the expletive was jarring and a little incongruous coming out of Lainey Madden. I wondered if she even realized she'd said it, as confused and angry and wrought up as she was.

"Maybe it was," I said. "What can you tell me about the threats?"

"Not very much. Chris couldn't imagine who was making them and neither could I. We thought it was one of those, you know, creeps who get their kicks from scaring women."

"It *was* a man who made the calls?"

"I think so. I listened in once on the bedroom extension; the voice was sort of muffled, but it sounded like a man."

"What did he say?"

"Just a lot of crazy stuff about getting Chris, making her pay for what she'd done to him. He never said what it was supposed to be that she'd done."

"The letters said the same kind of thing?"

"Pretty much. Do you want to see one of them?"

"You still have one? I understood you'd given them all to the police."

"I thought I had," she said. "But I found one I'd overlooked after they were gone. It's just like the others."

Lainey stood and disappeared through a doorway on the far side of the room. Half a minute later she came back and handed me a single sheet of inexpensive white paper business-folded into thirds.

I unfolded it. Typed in its approximate center was a sort of salutation and four short sentences; no signature of any kind. The typeface was pica and I could tell from the look of it that it belonged to a machine with a standard ribbon, rather than one of those newer carbon jobs. I could also tell that the typewriter was probably an older model: the "a" was tilted at a drunken angle and the upper curve of the "r" was chipped off at the top.

It read:

Ms. Christine Webster,

You are going to pay for what you did. One way or another, I promise you that. You bitch, I'll hurt you worse than you hurt me. I'll HURT you.

Creepy stuff, all right. The product of a sick mind. I refolded it and put it down on the coffee table. Lainey left it where it lay; she seemed not to want to touch it any more.

I said, "How many of these were there?"

"Six. They came about every other day."

"Where were they postmarked?"

"Here in the city."

"Did Christine contact the police about them?"

"Yes. But they said there wasn't anything they could do because he hadn't tried to *do* anything to her. Well, maybe he did do something to her," she said bitterly. "And now it's too late."

"Did she tell Jerry about the threats?"

"No. He would have quit his job and come down here to be with her, and she didn't want that; he couldn't be with her twenty-four hours a day. But she was going to tell him if they kept on much longer."

"You told the police she was thinking about seeing a private detective," I said. "When did she decide that?"

"Last week."

"Was my name mentioned at all?"

"No. And I don't know where she got your business card; I didn't even know she had it until the policemen asked me about it."

"Do you have any idea why she didn't get in touch with me?"

"I guess because she hadn't made up her mind yet. I told her seeing a detective was a good idea, but she thought it would cost too much; she didn't have much money."

It wouldn't have mattered to me, I thought. I would have tried to help if she'd come to me; I take jobs for the money but I don't turn them down, not this kind, because of a lack of it. God, why didn't she come to me?

Useless thinking again. I pushed the thoughts away and asked Lainey, "You're sure Christine had no personal enemies? Old boyfriends she'd broken up with, men she'd turned down, people she might have offended in some way?"

"I'm as sure as Chris was. Do you think her killer is someone she knew?"

"Yes," I said. "Unless she'd have gone out to Lake Merced at night to meet a stranger."

"I guess she probably wouldn't have. But she *was* a pretty trusting person, you know. And a kind person, too." Lainey shook her head. "She never hurt anybody, that's the thing. Oh, she was forever trying to tell people how to run their lives—but in a nice way, just trying to help them. She never hurt anybody."

"Had anything unusual happened to her recently, before the threats started? Anything she might have done or been involved in?"

Lainey gave that some thought. "No, I'm sure there wasn't," she said at length. "A girl she knew did commit suicide a little over a month ago, but that didn't have anything to do with Chris."

Suicide again. "What girl was that?"

"Her name was Bobbie Reid. She worked in the same building Chris did downtown—Chris had a part-time job with the Kittredge Advertising Agency—and they got to know each other."

"Were they close friends?"

"No. Chris didn't see her socially as far as I know."

"Why did Bobbie take her own life?"

"Chris said she was depressed about some sort of personal problem. One night she just swallowed a whole bottle of sleeping pills."

"Did Chris know what this personal problem was?"

"I think she did, but she didn't want to talk about it. She said Bobbie was dead and there was no use talking about the dead—" Lainey winced: Here we were talking about Christine and Christine herself was dead. "She could be kind of close-mouthed at times. Like she didn't tell me or Jerry she was pregnant until after she'd known it herself for weeks."

"Do you have any idea who Bobbie worked for?"

"No. The Kittredge Agency is in a big building in the Financial District and it must have at least a hundred offices in it."

"Is there anything else you can tell me about her?"

"That's all I know. Is it really important? I just don't see how her suicide could be connected with Chris' murder."

"Neither do I," I said. "But it's something that ought to be checked out, just in case. Did you tell the police about Bobbie Reid?"

"No, I don't think I did. It didn't occur to me then; I was pretty upset."

"I'll take care of it."

She nodded. And from outside, in the direction of the Medical Center, there was the faint shriek of a siren. Lainey cocked her head, listening to it—and shivered and hugged herself again. "Is it cold in here?" she said. "It feels cold."

"A little," I said, even though it wasn't. "I think I'd better be going. I don't have any more questions."

"All right. Will you let me know if you find out anything?"

"Of course."

"I won't be home for the weekend, though. I'm flying down to San Diego tonight. That's where Chris' parents live, you see, and the funeral is tomorrow." She wrapped her arms more tightly around herself. "I hope a lot of people come," she said. "Chris liked people."

The siren kept on wailing in the distance, like a discordant note in a dirge.

Or the scream of a young girl dying.

ELEVEN

I stopped for lunch at a cafe on Irving Street. Not because I wanted food; I had no appetite after the interview with Laincy Madden. But I had not eaten breakfast and my stomach was kicking up hunger pangs. It was already a quarter of one, and it seemed like an intelligent idea to give the digestive juices something to work on.

Over a tasteless hamburger and a cup of coffee I took my first look at what the *Chronicle* had to say about the murders. Both stories—a news report on the Carding homicide and an update on the death of Christine Webster—were on page two, the front page being given over to reports of trouble in the Middle East and a big Gay Rights march through Civic Center. There was suggestion of a possible link between the two cases and some attention was paid to Jerry Carding's mysterious disappearance from Bodega Bay; otherwise it was pretty straightforward stuff, no open speculation, just the basic facts. Martin Talbot was said to have confessed to the Carding murder, but the police were still investigating. My name was mentioned three or four times. There was even a paragraph on my career background in which I was referred to as "something of a Sam Spade type, the last of San Francisco's lone-wolf private eyes."

When I finished forcing down my hamburger I took the paper outside and deposited it in a trash receptacle. Then the last of San Francisco's lone-wolf private eyes got into his car and drove through the cold gray fog to S.F. State College.

There was no street parking near the Nineteenth Avenue entrance, so I turned into Park Merced and left the car in front of an apartment building on Cardenas. The woodsy campus, when I finally got onto it, was crowded but relatively quiet. It had not always been that way. I remembered the television footage from back in 1968: a student strike protesting the war in Vietnam and demanding a Third World Studies department and an open admissions policy; disruption and cancellation of classes, rock-throwing incidents; and our present U.S. senator, S.I. Hayakawa—then president of S.F. State—calling in the police riot squad to bust a few heads. Sad times back then. Ugly times. And all because of a war that we should have stayed the hell out of in the first place.

Well, things change—even for the better sometimes. The kids still looked the same, though, at least to my crusty old private eye: long hair and frizzed hair and Afros, beards, the kind of clothing my generation would have called Bohemian. Whatever happened to suits and ties and girls in winter outfits and summer dresses? The question made me smile mockingly at myself. Pining away for your lost youth, huh? I thought. You Sam Spade type, you. Come on, who cares what college students wear as long as they're happy and getting themselves an education? And most of these kids looked happy enough—maybe because it was Friday and they had the weekend and Thanksgiving vacation to look forward to, or because, for now anyway, all was right in their world.

But then I remembered that Christine Webster had been one

80

of them not too long ago, and I stopped smiling. She had no world anymore—not this one, at least. And neither did her unborn child.

I bypassed the Administration Building; I had already decided that there was no point in trying to locate Dave Brodnax through the Registrar's Office. College administrators are chary these days of giving out any information on students, including class schedules, and the fact that I was a detective would carry no weight at all. Lainey had said Brodnax was on the football team; I thought that maybe I would be able to get to him through the coach or somebody else in the Physical Education department.

As it turned out, finding Brodnax was easier than I had anticipated. The first young guy I stopped for directions told me the football team had just begun its daily practice in Cox Stadium; the last game of the season was tomorrow afternoon. He explained how to get to the stadium, over on the north side of the campus, and I made my way in that direction. Halfway there, I heard voices yelling the way football players do. They led me straight to the backside of a press box and an open gate in a cyclone fence.

Cox Stadium was laid out below in a kind of grotto, surrounded by wooded slopes, with more trees and undergrowth beyond the north end zone. Picturesque. The stands were made out of concrete and had rows of wooden benches; I was on the home side. I went through the gate and down fifty or sixty steps toward the field. The players, about four dozen of them in pads and practice jerseys and maroon helmets, were spread out across the turf running plays and banging into tackling dummies and doing wind sprints. The grass was pretty chewed up and deep furrows striped it where the yardlines were. It was not getting as much care as it should, probably because of maintenance cutbacks by the college when Proposition 13 limited their tax revenue.

I left the stands and crossed the track that ovaled the field and went to the sideline benches. A dark guy in his thirties was standing there, writing something on a clipboard. He wore a maroon windbreaker and had a whistle strung around his neck; I thought that he must be one of the coaches.

He glanced up as I approached him. It was cold down there and his cheeks had a brick-colored tinge. "Something I can do for you?"

"I'd like to see Dave Brodnax, if that's okay."

"Is it important?"

"Yes, sir, it is. Just tell him it's about Jerry Carding and Christine Webster."

The names seemed not to mean anything to him; maybe he only read the sports sections in the daily papers. But he said, "All right, I'll send him over," and moved away toward where a group of beefy-looking kids were just starting to practice the recovery of fumbles.

I watched him pick one out of the group, say something to him. The kid looked over at me, nodded at the coach, and then came trotting over. He took off his helmet just before he got to me, and I saw that he had a wild shock of reddish hair and two or three hundred freckles. He was at least four inches over six feet and would weigh in at around 240—some big kid. The knuckles on his hands looked as large as walnuts.

"Hi," he said, "I'm Dave Brodnax." His voice was surprisingly soft for someone his size, and it matched the look in his eyes: grave, troubled. "You another policeman?"

"Not exactly." I introduced myself. He knew my name from the newspapers and seemed willing enough to answer questions when I explained to him why I was investigating.

"But there's not much I can tell you," he said. "I don't have any idea who could've killed Christine or what happened to Jerry."

"The last time you talked to Jerry was when?"

"About a month ago when he and Steve came down from Bodega Bay for the weekend."

"Steve Farmer?"

"Right. Steve lives up there now, but his folks are here in the city. He brought Jerry down a few times, so he could visit them while Jerry was seeing Chris."

"Jerry doesn't have a car?"

"No. He did have one until last spring, but he sold it because he needed money to finish out the semester here at State."

"How did he get to San Francisco when Farmer didn't bring him?"

"Borrowed Steve's car or took the bus."

"Uh-huh. What was the job he had up there?"

"Deckhand on one of the commercial salmon boats," Brodnax said. "I don't know which one."

"Did he like doing that?"

"He thought it was okay. But it was just a way for him to make enough money so he could come back to school. He wants to be a writer, you know. One of those investigative reporters, like Woodward and Bernstein."

"Then as far as you know, he wasn't having any problems in Bodega Bay? Nothing that would make him drop out of sight as suddenly as he did?"

"Not as far as I know. I guess Steve could tell you if he was."

"Where does Farmer work?"

"At a place called The Tides. As a tally clerk and warehouseman at the fish market there."

I asked him about Jerry Carding's relationship with his father. His answers were pretty much the same as the ones Lainey Madden had given me: they'd got along fine, no major disagreements that Jerry had ever mentioned. Brodnax had met Victor Carding on a couple of occasions and professed a general liking for him, although "he was into booze kind of heavy and made some slurs about blacks once." And if he had disapproved of Christine for any reason, Brodnax did not know about it.

"I understand you introduced Jerry and Christine," I said then. "Is that right?"

"Yeah. She was in my psych class during the spring semester and I took her out a couple of times. But the vibes weren't right for anything heavy between us. She and Jerry connected right from the first; it seemed to be the real thing for both of them."

"Did you see much of her after she began going with Jerry?"

"Not too much. With Jerry a few times and around campus."

"Did she ever mention anything that might have been bothering her?"

"You mean those threats she'd been getting?" Brodnax shook his massive head. "I didn't know about them until the police told me. Chris never talked much about herself."

"Do you know the names Martin Talbot or Laura or Karen Nichols?"

"No. I didn't recognize them in the papers this morning and I still don't."

"How about Bobbie Reid?"

He frowned at that and shifted his helmet from one hand to the other. "Bobbie? What's she have to do with Chris' murder?"

"Maybe nothing, but her name came up. You knew her, then?"

"I met her a few times, yeah."

"Here at the college?"

"No. Steve Farmer used to go with her."

Now that was interesting. Christine and Bobbie knew each other, Bobbie used to date one of Jerry Carding's best friends, Bobbie commits suicide and Christine is murdered. Another connection—but where, if anywhere, did it lead?

I asked, "How long ago was this?"

"A year or so. They were pretty involved for a while."

"Why did they break up?"

"I don't know. Steve wouldn't say anything about it afterward; I don't think it was a friendly split."

"Was he hurt? Angry?"

"Both, I guess. But he got over it."

Did he? I wondered. "Did you see Bobbie at any time after the break-up?"

"No, not once."

"Do you know any of her other friends?"

"Just Steve."

"Jerry knew her, though?"

"Sure. Same way I did, through Steve."

"Did he ever talk about her?"

"I can't remember if he did."

"Why would she take her own life? Any ideas?"

"No. But she was a spacey chick."

"How do you mean?"

"Emotional, hyped up all the time."

"Drugs?"

"No," he said, "I don't think she was into that. A little pot, maybe, but that'd be all. She was just . . . I don't know, intense, freaky. Like she couldn't get her head together. I can't explain it any better than that."

The wind blowing across the floor of the stadium was bitter cold; I could feel my ears and cheeks burning. And I had run out of questions. So I said, "Okay, Dave, thanks. I won't keep you any longer."

He nodded solemnly. "I wish there was more I could do to help," he said. "I keep thinking something's happened to Jerry too. If he's all right, why hasn't he shown up all week? Or why hasn't somebody found him?"

"Somebody will, son. Sooner or later."

He nodded again and gave me his hand: his grip was as gentle as his voice. Then he put his helmet on and trotted onto the field, and I turned back toward the stands.

On the way there I noticed that the team's place-kicker had begun practicing field goals at the north end. He was a soccer-style kicker and pretty good, judging from the forty-yarder he put squarely between the uprights. The second kick I watched him try, from forty-five yards out, hit the crossbar, caromed straight up, hit the crossbar a second time, and fell through: good.

For some reason, my mind being what it is, that made me think of a country-and-western song that had been popular several years ago, a religious novelty item with the more or less unforgettable title of "Drop-Kick Me, Jesus, Through the Goal Posts of Life." Uh-huh. Well, some of us got drop-kicked through, all right. But some of us missed wide right or wide left, or just by inches, and some of us—like Christine Webster—got blocked at the line of scrimmage.

And then there were the ones like me. We made it through,

but not without hitting the damned crossbar a few times on the way. . . .

From the college I drove downtown and stopped at the main library in Civic Center where I spent half an hour looking through month-old issues of the *Chronicle* and *Examiner*. I found nothing at all about Bobbie Reid—no news story, no obituary, not even a funeral notice. Which meant that her death, like so many deaths in a city as large as San Francisco, had not been deemed important enough or unusual enough to warrant coverage; and that her body, like Christine Webster's, had been claimed by out-of-town relatives and her funeral held elsewhere.

There would have to be a police report on file, though, because the Homicide Detail is required by law to investigate all suicides. Eberhardt could look it up and use it to begin digging into Bobbie's background.

As for me, it seemed that a drive up to Bodega Bay was the next order of business. I had no leads to pursue here, no leads at all except for the tenuous link to Steve Farmer's involvement with Bobbie Reid; maybe I could find out something by talking to Farmer or by nosing around among the people in Bodega who knew Jerry Carding. On the way out of the library, I decided I would head up the coast first thing in the morning.

It was almost five o'clock by then. I had not been to my office all day and I had been out of touch since before eleven; it was possible that there was a message or two on my answering machine. Better check it out, I thought, and then call Eberhardt from there before he knocks off for the day.

Taylor Street was only a few blocks from the library, but it took me ten minutes to get there because of the rush-hour traffic. I coaxed the car into a narrow parking space near my building, went inside and looked through the slot in the mailbox. Nothing. The elevator was being cranky again: it made grinding noises and shuddered a lot on the way up. But it determined not to break down and strand me between floors, as it had once for twenty minutes a couple of years ago. I got out of it in a hurry, making a mental note to use the stairs until the landlord got the thing fixed again, and moved down the hall to the office door.

And pulled up short when I got to it.

The door was cracked open about six inches.

The skin along my back prickled; I could feel my stomach muscles begin to wire up. I had locked the door last night—I was always careful about locking it when I left the office because of the kind of neighborhood this was. The building had no janitor, and the only other person with a key would be the landlord; but he was not in the habit of paying uninvited calls on his tenants.

It was quiet in the hall except for the muffled, desultory clacking of a typewriter from one of the offices at the far end. But when I edged closer to the door I could hear another sound—a low pulsing beep, the kind a phone makes when it's been off the hook for more than thirty seconds. The slit between the door and jamb let me see nothing but darkness and the faint smeary glow from the lights in the building across the street.

I stayed where I was for another ten seconds, listening to the beep from the phone. Then I put the heel of my hand against the panel, held a breath, and gave the door a hard shove and went in across the threshold by one step, reaching out for the light switch on the inside wall.

There was nobody in the room or in the little alcove off of it; I could see that and sense the emptiness as soon as the overhead lights blazed. But what I did see made me recoil, stunned me with an impact that was almost physical.

The office had literally been torn apart.

TWELVE

Wanton, senseless destruction. All the drawers in the filing cabinets standing open and their contents strewn across the floor. The magazines from the table in the visitor's area ripped apart. The *Black Mask* poster pulled off the wall and shredded out of its frame. Everything swept off the desk, everything emptied out of the desk drawers. The typewriter still on its stand but the ribbon unwound from the spools like twenty feet of jumbled black intestine. The dregs from the coffee pot splashed on one wall; granules from the jar of instant coffee hurled around over the scattered papers. Jagged slash marks in the padded seat and back of my chair. Worms of white glue squeezed out over part of the desk and part of the client's chair. A long deep gouge in the desk top, made with a knife or maybe my letter opener. And in the alcove, all the supplies scraped off the shelves, my spare change of clothes cut into strips, and a can of cleanser sprinkled over the tangle on the floor.

I started to shake, looking at all of that. A savage, impotent rage welled up inside me; I had that ugly feeling you get when something like this happens, this kind of personal violation: a combination of pain and hatred and confusion that makes you want to smash something yourself.

The more I looked at the carnage in there, the wilder I felt. In self-defense I caught hold of the door, backed into the corridor, and shut out the sight of it. It was two or three minutes before the shaking stopped and the black haze cleared out of my head. Before I could trust myself to go talk to anybody.

The office across the hall was vacant and had been for weeks; I went back past the elevator, toward the clacking of the typewriter. A guy named Faber who ran a mail-order business had the office adjacent to mine, but there were no lights on inside and the door was locked. The fourth office, where the typewriter sounds were coming from, belonged to a CPA named Hadley. I opened the door and went in there.

Hadley was sitting at one of two desks across the room, hunt-and-pecking on a small portable. He looked up as I entered and gave me one of his smarmy grins. He was a thin bald-headed guy in his forties, with a fox-face and a wise-ass sense of humor.

"Well, if it isn't the dago private eye," he said. "How's the snooping business these days?"

"Knock it off, Hadley. I'm in no mood for bullshit."

He took a closer look at my face, and the grin wiped away in a hurry. "Hey," he said, "what's the matter with you? You look—" He stopped there, but he did not have to say it; we both knew how I looked.

"You see anybody at my office today?"

"No. Why?"

"Hear anything down there?"

"Like what?"

"Like noise. Like a lot of damn noise."

"I didn't hear any noise. What—"

"You been here all day?"

"No. I was out from eleven until about two."

"What about Faber across the hall? He come in today?"

"I don't think so; he usually doesn't on Fridays. Listen, what the hell happened?"

"Somebody busted up my office, that's what happened."

"Busted it up? You mean vandalized it?"

"That's what I mean."

Hadley began to look worried, but not for my sake. "You know who did it?"

"If I did, I wouldn't be here talking to you. You sure you didn't see anybody or hear anything while you were around?"

"Positive. Busted up your office, huh?" He looked around his own office, as if he were visualizing the same kind of thing happening here. "This building isn't safe any more," he said. "Raise the goddamn rent and it isn't even safe. Maybe we'd better think about moving out."

"Yeah," I said, "maybe we'd better."

I left him and went back along the hall to my door. When I opened it and bent to look at the lock I did not see any fresh scratches or signs of forced entry. But it wasn't much of a lock; a kid could have picked it with a bubblegum card. I got a tight hold on myself, stepped inside and shut the door behind me.

The destruction was not any easier to look at, but I could face it now without feeling as though I would come unglued. I stood still for a time and asked myself why. For God's sake, why?

Tenderloin junkie looking for money to buy a fix? Maybe. One of the tenants on the second floor had had his office broken into a few months ago and his petty-cash box looted, and there had been a couple of other break-ins over the years. But never my office, never a detective's; no money here, even a junkie knew that. Besides, what pawnable items there were, like the typewriter and the answering machine, had not been carried away.

Kids, vandals? More likely. Except that there were none of the vandal's trademarks: words spray-painted on the walls, puddles of urine or piles of feces. Except that pure vandalism was one of the few crimes that did not happen much in the Tenderloin, and especially not to one office in a building that was locked up at night and full of people during the day.

Somebody looking for something in my files? But I had no information that anyone could want, or at least none I could imagine anyone wanting; just a lot of case-report carbons, most of which were old and nearly all of which were mundane. That sort of thief, looking for something he couldn't find, might take out his frustration on the office itself—only this was not an act of frustration. It had taken time, a lot of time, to do all this damage. And that made it an act of frenzy, done by somebody with—

—a sick mind. And whoever had been threatening Christine Webster, who had maybe killed her, had a sick mind; the anonymous letter Lainey Madden had shown me confirmed that. The same person? Possible—and yet it didn't seem to make much sense. Why come after me? My involvement was minimal enough and I knew even less and posed a far smaller threat than the police. And what would destroying my office accomplish in any case?

Still. The time was right: somebody vandalizes the office while I'm in the middle of two linked murder cases. It could be one of the people I had met and talked to in the past few days. Or it could be somebody I had yet to meet and talk to; my name had been all over the papers. Jerry Carding? Steve Farmer?

Somebody.

Why?

The beeping from the disabled phone penetrated and sent me wading through the debris on the floor, around to the far side of the desk. The phone was lying there in two pieces, the receiver hooked over one of the chair legs. I picked it up and put it back together and set it down on the slashed chair seat. The answering machine was upside-down under the window; I picked that up too and laid it on top of the typewriter.

I dialed the Hall of Justice and asked for Eberhardt. Got him half a minute later. "It's me again," I said.

"Now what? I was just on my way home."

I told him what now. There was a silence. Then he said,

"Christ, can't you stay out of trouble for one day?" but he no longer sounded annoyed or irascible.

"Lecture me some other time, will you? This isn't my fault."

"Bad, huh?"

"It couldn't be much worse."

"You think it's connected with the Webster and Carding cases?"

"I don't know what to think. Maybe."

"All right. I'll be there in twenty minutes."

"Bring a couple of lab boys with you. There might be prints."

"Twenty minutes."

I hung up and fiddled with the switches on the answering machine. It seemed to be working okay—and there was a message on it, from Donleavy. His voice said I should call him at his office in Redwood City and then proceeded to give the number.

The message told me something else, too: my office had been vandalized sometime today, during business hours. If it had happened last night Donleavy would not have been able to reach me because of the disabled phone.

I dialed his number right away; it was better to be doing something constructive than brooding at what was left of this place. And it turned out that he was also still in.

"Thought you'd want to know," he said. "I had a couple of my men make another search of the Carding garage and the grounds around it; they found the second bullet."

"Good. Where?"

"Outside the garage window, in a bush."

"So that's what happened to it. Sure, the window was part way open, now that I think about it; I should have remembered that before. You going to withdraw the charges against Talbot now?"

"Not yet. Chances are he fired the bullet through the open window, considering where it was found and a Ballistics report confirming that it came from the murder weapon; but there's no way of proving he did. Carding could have fired it himself, sometime prior to his death."

"But you do believe Talbot is innocent?"

Donleavy made a sighing sound. "What I believe doesn't seem to hold much water around here. The DA's still planning to prosecute."

"Has Talbot's condition changed any?"

"Status quo. He's been under sedation most of the day. That's a preliminary treatment in cases of suicidal depression, the doctors tell me."

"No other developments, I guess?"

"Nope. How about with you? I talked to Laura Nichols this afternoon at the hospital; she said she'd hired you to do some investigating of your own."

"Yeah. I was going to call you about that tonight. You mind?"

"Your buddy Eberhardt doesn't mind. Why should I?"

I told him about Bobbie Reid and her connection with Christine Webster and Jerry Carding. "Might be something in that, at least where the Webster case is concerned; I'll pass it along to Eberhardt. I don't see how it could tie in with the Carding homicide, though."

"Neither do I," Donleavy said. "Anything else?"

"My office was vandalized today. Torn apart. I'm standing here in the wreckage right now, waiting for Eberhardt."

"Rough. Any idea who did it?"

"No. But I'm not so sure it's coincidence."

"How come?"

"Nothing stolen, for one thing. What time did you leave your message on my machine?"

"About eleven. Why?"

"Whoever did it knocked the phone off the hook," I said. "So it had to have happened sometime between your call and when I got here a little after five. Which pretty much lets out street kids; they don't vandalize business offices in broad daylight."

"So you think it ties in with the two homicide cases?"

"That's what I'm afraid of."

After we rang off I looked around at the destruction again, in spite of myself. My gaze settled on the shredded *Black Mask* poster. It was no special loss; I could get another one made from the magazine cover. But it made me think of my collection of pulps. The damage here would amount to no more than a few hundred dollars—but what if the same kind of thing happened at my flat? Those six thousand pulps had to be worth more than thirty thousand dollars at the current market prices; most were irreplacable, at least where I was concerned, and I had damned little personal property insurance. The thought of them being demolished started me shaking all over again.

I got on the horn to Dennis Litchak, a retired fire captain who lives below me, and asked him to go upstairs and check on my flat; we had exchanged keys sometime ago, as a general precaution between neighbors. He was gone the better part of ten minutes and I did a lot of fidgeting while I waited. But when he came on again he said, "Everything's okay. You didn't have any visitors."

I let out a breath. "Thanks, Dennis."

"What's up, anyhow?"

"I'll tell you about it later."

I went over to the window and stood looking down at the misty lights along Taylor Street. The pulps were still in my mind. My flat was not nearly so easy to get into as this office, but it was a long way from being impregnable; sooner or later, somebody could get inside and destroy or even steal those magazines. That was a fact and I had damned well better pay attention to it. Have another lock put on the front door and the back door. And increase my personal property insurance right away, no matter how much it cost for the premiums. And then just hope to God I did not come home someday to find what I had found here.

A couple of minutes passed. Then two cars pulled up at the curb below—Eberhardt's Dodge and an unmarked police sedan—and Eb and two other guys got out and entered the building. I returned to the desk and cocked a hip against one corner of it, where there were none of the drying worms of white glue. Pretty soon I heard the grinding of the elevator, then their steps in the hall, and the door opened and they came in.

Eberhardt took one long look at the office and said, "Jesus Christ."

"I told you it was bad."

"Looks like a psycho job," one of the other guys said. He had a field-lab case in one hand. "Somebody doesn't like you worth a damn."

"Yeah."

While the lab boys went to work, picking their way through the mess on the floor, I stepped into the hall with Eberhardt. He said then, "Hell of a thing to walk into. You okay, *paisan?*"

"More or less."

"Don't make a grudge deal out of it, huh?"

"You know me better than that, Eb. Besides, if anybody finds out who did it, it'll be you. Or Donleavy, maybe."

"If there's a connection."

"The more I think about it, the more likely it seems."

"We'll see."

"Did your man find out anything new in Bodega?"

"Nothing positive," he said. "The Carding kid left all of his belongings behind when he disappeared, but that may not mean much; none of what little stuff there is is worth anything. And if anybody up there knows where he is or why he left, they're not talking. Friend of his, Steve Farmer, did say that he'd been kind of secretive for a few days. Maybe writing an article of some kind; that's what Farmer thinks."

I remembered Lainey Madden saying that Jerry had not come down to San Francisco last weekend for that same apparent reason. I said, "Farmer didn't have any idea what this article might be about?"

"No. There wasn't any sign of it among Jerry's effects, either."

"Well, I'm going up there tomorrow myself. Maybe I can nose up something. Okay with you?"

"Go ahead. But it'll probably be a waste of time."

"I know. One thing I can do, though, is ask Farmer about a girl named Bobbie Reid. He used to date her, and she was also a friend of Christine Webster's. She committed suicide about a month ago, because of some sort of personal problem."

Eberhardt cocked an eyebrow. "You find all that out today?"

"Yes. From Lainey Madden and Dave Brodnax."

"You can be a pretty good cop when you set your mind to it," he said without irony. "What else do you know about this Reid girl?"

I filled him in on what few other details I had learned. "The suicide report ought to tell you her next-of-kin," I said, "and maybe who some of her other friends were."

"I'll have Klein check it out."

It was another fifteen minutes before one of the lab guys put his head out and said they were finished. Eberhardt and I went back inside. Most of the file papers and folders had been gathered up into loose stacks, and the rest of the wreckage had been stirred around in a methodical sort of way; the desk and chairs and file cabinets and a few other things had a fine dusting of fingerprint powder on them.

"We found two dominant sets of latents," one of the lab boys said, "but one set is bound to be yours. Are your prints on file with the Department?"

"Yes."

"Okay. We'll just have to hope the other set is on file too—somewhere. And that they belong to whoever laid into this place."

"How long will it take to run a check?"

"Not too long, local and state. If we have to go to the FBI," he said wryly, "it could take days."

Eberhardt said, "Call him at home later tonight or first thing in the morning, either way. I'll give you the number."

"Right."

"Anything else?"

"Not much," the other guy said. "Lock on the door wasn't jimmied; probably picked with a credit card or something. Smudges on a couple of the papers that seem to be oxblood shoe polish. No help in that, though, unless it's a rare brand that can be traced to certain dealers." He shrugged. "And that's it."

The three of them left not long afterward. When they were gone I spent some time scraping the dried glue off the desktop, putting things back into the drawers. But my heart wasn't in it. It would take me at least a day to sweep up the floors, scrub the walls and furniture, sort out the files, get somebody to cart away the slashed chair and somebody else to bring in a new one. Next week—when some of the pain and anger had dulled and I could face the task with a sense of detachment.

I got out of there at eight-thirty. And home a little before nine. I forced myself to eat a sandwich I did not want and thought about calling Laura Nichols; but I had nothing of substance to report and no desire to talk to her in any event. I did call Dennis Litchak again, to tell him I would be away tomorrow and to ask him to check on the flat for me from time to time. He said he would.

At a quarter of ten, just as I was about to head into the shower, the phone rang. It was one of the lab guys: they had run the second set of latent prints through the state and local computers. No card match, no ID. Whoever the prints belonged to had never been fingerprinted in the state of California.

Terrific.

So I took my shower and went to bed and eventually to sleep. And had a nightmare about coming home, opening the front door, and being inundated by toppling stacks of pulp magazines, all of which had been ripped to pieces. Voices kept screaming accusations at me, saying things like, "Look what you've done to us! You're supposed to be the last of the lone-wolf private eyes; why didn't you protect your own kind?" Then the voices became eyes, thousands of eyes that glared balefully at me while I fought to keep from drowning in a sea of shredded pulp paper.

It was absurd stuff, of course, with comic overtones. But it scared hell out of me just the same.

THIRTEEN

Until the early sixties Bodega Bay had been a quiet and old-fashioned commercial fishermen's province. People from the bigger Sonoma County towns like Santa Rosa and Petaluma went there to buy fresh crabs and other seafood, or to use one of the nearby beaches, and families came up from San Francisco once in a while to take in the scenic beauty of the Sonoma coastline; otherwise the natives had the place pretty much to themselves.

But then Hitchcock filmed his suspense movie, *The Birds*, on and around the bay, at the village of Bodega close by, and at the complex of bayfront buildings called The Tides and that resulted in a good deal of publicity and national prominence. Before long Bodega Bay became something of an "in" place to visit or even to live at, and it began to change accordingly. Along with streams of sightseers in the spring and summer months, artists of one type or another, enterprising merchants, retired couples, sport fishermen after salmon or sea bass all flocked there; land developers built a couple of fancy motels and at least one expensive community of homes, called Bodega Bay Harbor; antique and souvenir shops sprang up everywhere. Today, less than two decades later, it was a different place. The rugged coastline was still the same, and most of the old buildings and landmarks along Highway 1 were still there, but all the charm and attractiveness seemed to be gone. The impression you got was one of creeping suburbia: another twenty years and all the hills and cliffs and beaches would probably be covered with houses, fast-food franchises, shopping centers.

That was the feeling I had, anyway, when I got up there a few minutes past noon on Saturday—my first visit to Bodega Bay since a Sunday outing with Erika Coates eight years ago, in the good days before the breakup of our relationship. But then, maybe part of the feeling was my mood, and part of it, too, the heavy low-hanging fog that shrouded the coast and gave everything new and old a cheerless aspect. The mist was so thick it was almost like rain; I had to use my windshield wipers since passing through Valley Ford ten miles back.

I turned off the highway into the parking lot around which The Tides was built. There were only three other cars in the lot and nobody out and around that I could see; even the road was more or less deserted. I parked in front of the Wharf Bar and Restaurant and got out into the fog and an icy wind.

This place, at least, did not appear to have changed much. All the same buildings—The Tides Motel, the small ice house, the Union 76 dock, the barber shop and souvenir shop—and all of them still painted white with garish orange roofs and trim. Even the weathered signs on the front of The Tides Wharf, a long low structure that housed the restaurant and a fresh-fish market, looked to be the same.

I went over and onto the pier that led around and along the Wharf's backside. The bay was an oily grayish-black color, wind-rumpled into whitecaps; the red-and-white buoys that marked the crossing channel and three high-masted fishing boats, anchored downwind, rocked in the swells. You could not see much of Bodega Head across the bay, and the narrows that led into the ocean at the southern end, bounded by a pair of rock jetties, were all but obliterated. The sea air smelled sharply of salt and dark rain: another storm building somewhere out on the Pacific.

An archway opened off the pier into the warehouse area where fish-market employees weighed, cleaned, and packaged catches brought in by the commercial boats. On my right as I walked through were round concrete tanks used to keep shellfish fresh; the long room to my left was lined with wooden benches and cluttered with large carts on oversized metal wheels, small dollies, stacks of wooden pallets, rows of storage lockers, a Toledo weighing scale, and two big refrigeration units.

At the far end a young guy dressed in a sweatshirt and Levi's was hosing down the concrete floor. As I approached he turned and then released the hand shut-off on the hose. He had intense brown eyes, a square flattish face, and a mop of light-brown hair parted in the middle and swept back over his ears. Across the front of his sweatshirt, in maroon letters, were the words *San Francisco State College*.

"Steve Farmer?" I asked him.

He gave me a somewhat wary look. "That's right."

I told him my name. "I'd like to ask you a few questions about Jerry Carding, if you don't mind."

"You're that private detective, aren't you. The one in the papers."

"Yes."

The wariness went away; his eyes took on a worried, unhappy look. He dropped the hose, ran a hand through his shaggy hair. "Well, I can't help you much. I don't know what happened to Jerry; I've already told the police that. But one thing's sure: he didn't disappear because Chris got pregnant *or* because he had anything to do with her murder. He loved her; they were planning to get married. And he's a nonviolent person. He couldn't harm another human being, not for *any* reason."

I nodded. "Everyone I've talked to says essentially the same thing."

"Don't you believe it?"

"I'd like to. When did you last talk to Jerry?"

Farmer sighed. "The day before he disappeared. Last Saturday. We had a beer together after work."

"What did you talk about?"

"Nothing much. He was in a hurry to get home."

"Home?"

"I mean the Darden house over in Bodega. That was where he was living."

"Did he say why?"

"No. Just that he had some work to do."

"The article you told the police about?"

"I think so."

"Did he ever hint as to what it might be about?"

"Never. But he seemed to think it was important."

"How long had he been working on it?"

"I don't know. He'd been kind of excited for three or four days, though."

"Excited in what way? Nervous? Eager?"

"Eager," Farmer said. "When I asked him about it he said it was a secret and I'd find out when everybody else did."

"Who're his other friends here? Anyone he might have talked to about what he was writing?"

"Just Sharon Darden, I guess. Her mother owns the house where Jerry lived; she rents out one of her rooms. But I talked to Sharon after Jerry vanished; she doesn't know anything more than I do."

"How close were she and Jerry?"

"If you mean were they making it together, the answer is no. I told you, Jerry was in love with Chris. He's not the kind of guy who screws around on his lady."

"I just wondered if they were good friends."

"Pretty good. If Jerry'd told her anything, she'd have mentioned it to me or the police. She wouldn't have any reason to keep it to herself."

"When did you first find out Jerry was missing?"

"Monday morning. Gus Kellenbeck called me because Jerry hadn't reported for work."

"Kellenbeck?"

"He owns the Kellenbeck Fish Company," Farmer said. "Jerry did odd jobs for him."

"Oh? I thought he worked as a deckhand."

"He did, off and on. But he couldn't make enough money doing that, so he went to work for Kellenbeck."

"This fish company is where?"

"A little ways north of here, on the highway."

"Is it open on Saturdays?"

"Yeah. Every day but Sunday."

"Which boat did Jerry work on?"

"The *Kingfisher*. Andy Greene's troller."

"And where would I find Greene?"

"Over at the marina, probably. On the other side of the bay. He lives on board the *Kingfisher*."

I asked him about Victor Carding, and got a replay of the unenlightening answers Lainey Madden and Dave Brodnax had given me. Then Farmer paused, frowned, and asked:

"Do the police think Jerry had something to do with what happened to his old man? Is that why you're asking about him?"

"It's a possibility."

"Not to me, it isn't. I thought they arrested the guy who shot Mr. Carding; that's what the papers said."

"Martin Talbot isn't guilty," I said.

"He confessed, didn't he?"

"Yes. But he's not guilty. There are psychological reasons why somebody would confess to a crime he didn't commit."

Farmer half-turned and stared over at one of the refrigerator units. After a time he said, "How can anything like this happen?" but he seemed to be talking more to himself than to me. "Jerry's mother dead in an accident, his father murdered, Chris murdered—everybody he cared about just . . . wiped out. What if he's dead too?"

Yeah, I thought. What if he's dead too?

He faced me again. "Jerry's not a killer, he's a victim. You understand? He's a victim whether he's all right or not."

"I understand, son."

102

He seemed suddenly a little embarrassed, as if he felt he had displayed too much emotion in front of a stranger. "Look, I, uh, I've got work to do. Is there anything else?"

"Just a couple of things. Is Martin Talbot's name familiar to you?"

"No. I never heard of him until yesterday."

"How about Laura Nichols? Karen Nichols?"

"No."

"About Christine—did she have any enemies you might know about?"

"You mean somebody who'd make those threats the paper said she'd been getting?" He shook his head. "No. Whoever that crazy bastard is, he must be the one who killed her."

"So it would seem," I said. And then asked him the question I had been saving for last: "What can you tell me about Bobbie Reid?"

His reaction was immediate: he jerked slightly, as if I had swatted him one, and his face closed up and something flickered in his eyes that might have been pain. "What does Bobbie have to do with any of this?"

"I don't know that she has anything to do with it. But she and Chris were friends."

"The hell they were."

"You didn't know that? It's true, Steve."

"Bobbie's dead," he said stiffly. "She killed herself more than a month ago."

"So I've been told. Do you know why?"

"No." But he said the word a little too fast, it seemed to me. "Listen, I don't want to talk about Bobbie, okay?"

"You'll have to talk to somebody about her sooner or later. If not me, then the police."

"She couldn't have anything to do with what happened to Chris. How could she? No—I've got enough dead people to think about as it is."

I wanted to press him further, but it would not have done any good; his expression said that he was not going to do any more talking no matter what I said. "All right, Steve. Have it your own way. Thanks for your time."

He was no longer looking at me. He said, "Yeah," and bent to pick up the hose. I watched him walk away from me, open the nozzle, and begin to wash the floor again. But this time he did it in hard, jerky sweeps, with the stream of water thinned down to a jet.

I went out and down the corridor between the fish market and the restaurant. My hands and feet were cold; I decided on a cup of coffee before I made any more stops.

Inside the restaurant I sat near the windows overlooking the bay and did some brooding while I waited for one of the waitresses to serve me. Steve Farmer seemed like a decent enough kid, and his concern for Jerry Carding had struck me as genuine. But I was pretty sure he had lied about not knowing or at least suspecting the motive for Bobbie Reid's suicide. Why? Deep personal feelings that had nothing to do with murder? Or for reasons that did have something to do with murder?

I wondered if Farmer had lied about anything else, or held back information of some kind. I wondered if the relationships between the young people in this business were what they seemed to be. Add all those questions to the dozen or so others that had accumulated, shuffle them together with the known facts, and what did you get?

Nothing.

So far, not a damned thing.

FOURTEEN

There was not much to the village of Bodega—just a grocery store, a post office, a tavern, a garage-and-filling station, a few more antique stores than I remembered, and an old country church. I had neglected to ask Steve Farmer how to get to the Darden house, so I stopped in at the grocery to ask directions. The woman there said the Darden place was up on the hill above the village, lots of ice plants out front, can't miss it.

When I drove up past the church I discovered that it *wasn't* a church, not any more; it was a galleria dispensing local artwork. Sign of the times. And of what had happened to the Bodega Bay area. The old values, the old traditions, did not seem to mean much any more. At least not to those who worshipped at the shrine of the Almighty Buck.

The road curled around behind the galleria and wound upward along the face of the hill. From there on a clear day you would have a fine view toward the ocean; now, all you could make out through the screen of fog were vague surrealistic outlines, like backgrounds in a dream.

The Darden house turned out to be a rambling two-story structure at least as old as I was. The ice plants in the fenced-in yard gave the place a good deal of color: vermillion and lavender and pink, all glistening wetly in the mist. I parked in front, climbed out, and went through the gate and up a crushed shell path to the porch.

Just as I reached it, a slender attractive woman in her mid-forties came around one corner on a branch of the shell path. She wore a scarf over short graying hair, a pair of man's dungarees, and a heavy plaid lumberman's jacket; in her right hand were several sprigs of rosemary. She smiled when she saw me—a nice smile, friendly, infectious.

"Hello there," she said. "Something I can do for you?"

I returned the smile. "Mrs. Darden?"

"Yes?"

Her expression sobered when I showed her the photostat of my license and told her why I was there; a troubled sadness came into her hazel eyes. It was the kind of sadness you see in people who have faced tragedy and known sorrow in their own lives. She had lost someone close to her once, I thought. Her husband, maybe. Farmer had implied that she and her daughter were the only two Dardens who lived here; and she was still wearing her wedding ring.

"It's terrible," she said, "what's happened to Jerry's family and fiance. Just awful."

"Yes, ma'am."

"I just hope that . . . well, that no harm has come to Jerry too." She sighed and shook her head. "His disappearance is a complete mystery to us. To my daughter Sharon and me, I mean."

"Would your daughter be home now?"

"No, I'm afraid not. She's gone to Santa Rosa for the day with her young man." Mrs. Darden paused. "Come inside, won't you? It's much too cold to talk here."

She led me into the house and then into a parlor appointed with forties-style furniture and an odd combination of feminine and masculine objects: hand-painted glass paperweights and a rack of well-used pipes; porcelain figurines and an old cavalry sword hanging above the fireplace mantel; oval cameo portraits in delicate frames and an oil painting of a square-rigged clipper ship. I declined her invitation of something to drink, waited until she had shed her coat and the sprigs of rosemary and seated herself in a padded Boston rocker, and put myself down on the couch.

I asked, "When did you last see Jerry, Mrs. Darden?"

"The night he disappeared. Around nine o'clock."

"What was his mood?"

"Oh, he seemed very excited—very intense. He'd been in his room all day, working; he didn't even join us for meals."

"He was writing something, is that right?"

"Yes," she said. "He'd borrowed Sharon's typewriter a few days before and I could hear it clacking away during the evenings and all day Sunday. I asked him what he was writing, and so did Sharon, but he wouldn't tell us. He was just like a little boy with a secret."

"When he left the house, was it on foot?"

"Yes."

"Alone?"

"Oh yes."

"Did he say where he was going?"

"To the post office, he told Sharon. He had two envelopes with him."

"What sort of envelopes?"

"Large manila ones."

"Both stamped and addressed?"

"Only one, I believe. Seems to me the other was blank."

"Did you or Sharon notice the name on the addressed one?"

"No, we didn't."

"I understand the police found nothing helpful among Jerry's belongings," I said. "No carbon of what he'd been writing, no discarded papers of anything like that."

"Nothing at all, no."

"Did they take his things away with them?"

"They didn't seem to feel that was necessary. I've left everything in Jerry's room, just as it was. We're still hoping he'll come back."

"Would it be all right if I looked through them?"

"Surely. I was just going to suggest that you do."

She took me upstairs, into a spacious room at the rear of the house. Jerry Carding had added no personal touches to the furnishings, except for a stack of books on the writing desk set between the room's two windows, and a framed photograph of Christine Webster on the nightstand. The photo gave me a cold hollow feeling: I had only known her in death.

The rest of Jerry's belongings did not amount to much, as Eberhardt had said. Enough clothing to fit into the suitcase in the closet, all of it casual, mod-styled and inexpensive. A pair of sneakers and a pair of old fisherman's boots. A cheap pocket calculator. A packet of wheatstraw cigarette papers, the kind kids use nowadays to roll marijuana joints. So maybe he smokes a little grass, I thought. So what?

So nothing.

I looked at the books on the writing desk. Dictionary, thesaurus, college journalism text, a couple of novels, and the rest a selection of popular accounts of investigative reporting. There was nothing hidden between the pages of any of them; the cops would have found it if there had been.

The typewriter was an old Smith-Corona manual that had seen a lot of wear. Beside it were several sheets of white dime-store paper. On a hunch I took one of the sheets, rolled it into the platen, and typed out the words "Jerry Carding" with one forefinger. But the "a" key was not tilted and the "r" key was not chipped; the threatening letters to Christine Webster had not been written on this machine.

I lifted the typewriter and looked at the rubber pad underneath. All that was there besides some dust was a small corner torn off a piece of thin paper. But not typing or book paper; the corner was glossy and colored brown with a line of black. I picked it up and took a closer look. Off a label of some kind, I thought. Or maybe a decal. The back of the glossy side was gummed.

I held it out to Mrs. Darden on the tip of my finger. "Can you guess what this might have come from?"

She peered at it. "I'm afraid not, no."

It may or may not have had any significance; I decided I ought to keep it just in case and put it into my shirt pocket.

We went downstairs again. In the foyer I said, "Would you mind if I came back and spoke to your daughter?"

"Of course not," Mrs. Darden said. "But I'm afraid Sharon won't be back from Santa Rosa until late this evening."

I had already given some thought to spending the night in Bodega Bay; it seemed like a reasonable idea, assuming I did not turn up anything conclusive in the next couple of hours. I said, "I think I'll probably stay over until tomorrow. I could drop by again in the morning."

"That would be fine. You could come around ten-thirty, we'll be home from church by then."

"Thanks, Mrs. Darden."

"Not at all," she said gravely. "Sharon and I both want to do everything we can to help."

The Kellenbeck Fish Company was a long narrow red-roofed building set at a perpendicular angle to the shore, so that most of it extended out into the bay on thick wooden pilings. A salt-grayed sign hanging below the eaves in front stated its name and said that Gus Kellenbeck was owner and proprietor. There were a couple of ancient, corroded hoists off to one side of a gravel parking area; wedged in between them was a dusty green Cadillac. One other vehicle, a well-traveled Ford pick-up, sat with its nose at an angle to the highway.

I took my car in alongside the pick-up, got out and went to a shedlike enclosure built onto the front of the main structure. The door there was locked. So I walked around to the side, where a narrow catwalk followed the building's length. The catwalk took me onto a dock about fifty yards square, with a pier in somewhat ramshackle condition attached to it. The pier jutted another fifty or sixty yards into the bay; a lone salmon troller was tied up at the end of it, bobbing in the choppy water.

A middle-aged guy was doing something with a seine net near a row of iron crab pots. I crossed to him and asked where I might find Gus Kellenbeck.

"His office," the guy said laconically. "Inside."

I went into the building through a pair of open hangar-type doors made out of corrugated iron. The warehouse was cluttered with much the same type of equipment and storage facilities as inside The Tides Wharf, except that there was more of it. A bank of machinery, with a crisscross of conveyor belts fronting it, took up a portion of the wall at the upper end. On my left was a cubicle that would be the office; a single grime-streaked window was set beside a closed door. I could not see inside it from the entrance.

The wooden floor was wet and slippery with fish scales; I picked my way across it to the cubicle. When I knocked on the door a hoarse voice said, "What is it?"

I opened the door and looked in. A short bearish guy sat behind a desk cluttered with papers and junk, an open ledger book in front of him and a pencil tucked over his right ear. There was also a bottle of Canadian whiskey on the desk, along with a glass half-full of liquor. The guy glanced at me, glanced at the bottle, scowled, and put his hands flat on the ledger book. He did not look too happy to have a stranger find him drinking on the job, even if he did own the place.

"Mr. Kellenbeck?"

"Yeah?"

"Okay if I come in? I'd like to talk to you."

"What about?"

"Jerry Carding."

That made him scowl again. But he waved an admitting hand at me, closed the ledger, and got up on his feet. He was thick-featured and olive-complexioned, with blue-black hair that was a snarl of ringlets; his nose had been broken at least once, and improperly set, and it seemed to list at a forty-five degree angle toward the left side of his face. His eyes, sea-green flecked with yellow, were heavy-lidded and bloodshot.

I went in and shut the door behind me. Kellenbeck watched me come over in front of the desk; he still did not look happy. He said, "You a policeman?"

"No. Private investigator."

When I gave him my name he said, "Oh, yeah," and then scowled a third time. "How come you're here? I thought the cops were handling the kid's disappearance."

"They are. But I'm working for Martin Talbot's sister. With police sanction."

"Police sanction, huh? All right, sit down."

I took the only other chair in the office, Kellenbeck plunked himself down again in his swivel chair, pinched the bridge of his nose as if he had a headache, and looked at the bottle again. A moment later he caught it up by its bare neck and put it away inside one of the desk drawers.

"So what do you want to know?" he said.

"Well, do you have any idea where Jerry might have gone?"

"Assuming he didn't do any killings, you mean?"

"Assuming that."

He shrugged. "Where do kids go these days? They spend a little time someplace, pretty soon they move on like—what do you call them?"

"Nomads?"

"Yeah. Like nomads."

"Except that Jerry didn't take any of his belongings with him," I said.

"No? I didn't know that."

"Did you see him last Sunday, Mr. Kellenbeck?"

"No. Saturday was the last time, when he knocked off for the day."

"Did he say anything to you then? Give you any indication he might be planning to go away?"

"Not a word," Kellenbeck said. He took a short greenish cigar from a humidor on his desk and began to unwrap it. "I was kind of surprised when he didn't show up on Monday morning, because he'd never missed a day before and always came in right on time. So I called up the Dardens, where he was living, and that friend of his, Steve something, works down at The Tides. Trying to get in touch with him, you know? But he'd just taken off without telling nobody where he was going."

"May I ask when you pay your employees?"

"Middle of the week. Wednesdays."

"Did Jerry ask you for his wages on Saturday?"

"No, why?"

"Well, he had three days pay coming," I said. "Seems a little odd that he didn't ask for it if he was planning to leave Bodega Bay the following night. He's not a wealthy kid; he'd need money wherever he was going."

Kellenbeck scowled one more time. "I never thought of that," he said. He lit his cigar with a wooden kitchen match. "Maybe he wasn't planning to leave on Saturday. Maybe he only got it into his head the next day."

"Maybe. But what would make him decide to go that suddenly, without waiting to collect his salary?"

"You got me. I can't figure it."

"Did he mention anything to you about an article he was writing?"

"Article? You mean like the one he did on salmon fishing?"

"Something he was working on before he disappeared."

"What would that be?"

"I don't know. That's what I'm trying to find out."

"First I heard of it," Kellenbeck said. "He never said a word to me about writing anything."

"Do you know if he had trouble with anyone around here?"

"What kind of trouble?"

"A fight or an argument of some kind. Like that."

"If he did, I never heard about it. He got along with everybody, far as I know. An easygoing kid."

I asked a few more questions and learned nothing from Kellenbeck's answers that I did not already know. When I got up to leave he stood, too, and put out his hand; I took it. He said, "Anything else I can do, you let me know."

"I'll do that," I said, and left him chewing on his cigar and eyeing the glass of whiskey that was still on his desk.

The wind cut at me in icy gusts when I came out onto the dock. Overhead, low-flying tendrils of mist sailed inland at a pretty good clip, but out over the ocean the fog had lifted somewhat and you could see the black-rimmed clouds above it. The day had turned darker, colder; the bay was frothed with whitecaps now, and the smell of salt and ozone had sharpened. It would not be long before the storm blew in and the rains came.

And where is he? I thought. What happened last Sunday night?

What happened to Jerry Carding?

FIFTEEN

The road that curled around the northern lip of the bay was relatively new and in good condition; but it was also slick with mist, and the tires on my car were starting to bald a little. I drove at a circumspect twenty-five, squinting through the arcs made by my clattering windshield wipers.

Erika and I had taken this road, I remembered, on that long-ago Sunday outing. It followed the bay's edge toward the jetty and then hooked back up to the top of Bodega Head. From up there you could watch the surf hammering at the jagged rocks below; and you could see the excavation scars where the government had begun work on a proposed nuclear power plant twenty years ago. A public hue and cry had kept them from going through with their plans: this was earthquake country and nobody wanted to be sitting in the shadow of a nuclear reactor if a big quake hit. We had talked about that, Erika and I, standing

114

up there on the Head, holding hands like a couple of young lovers. And later we had gone back to The Tides to eat crab cioppino before driving home to San Francisco. And that night, after we had finished making love, Erika had said jokingly, "You know something, old bear? You make the earth shake pretty good yourself."

Bittersweet memories . . .

The marina for both commercial and pleasure craft was located in the northwest corner of the harbor, opposite several scattered cottages and homes built along the lower slopes of Bodega Head. It was fairly small and laid out like a squared-off letter W— three long board floats with slips flanking each of them, separated by narrow channels but connected on the shoreward end by a walkway. Less than a dozen boats were moored there now, most of them commercial trollers.

I eased my car onto the shoulder near somebody's driveway, crossed the road, and stepped onto the ramp that led out to the slips. The wind was strong enough here to numb my cheeks and make my eyes water; above the sound of it you could hear the boats rubbing and banging against the floats. They all seemed deserted at first, but when I reached the ramp's end I noticed movement on one off to my right, in a slip two-thirds of the way along the nearest float. I peered over there. The lettering on the stern read *Kingfisher*, and below that, *Bodega Bay*.

I climbed down a short metal ladder onto the swaying float and made my way carefully along the boards. A stocky well-muscled guy dressed in denim trousers and a thin sweatshirt, no coat, was kneeling on deck; long copper-colored hair fanned out in the wind behind him like a horse's mane at full gallop. He had the engine housing up, and there was an open tool box and an assortment of wrenches and things laid out on a strip of canvas beside him. I had a glimpse of the engine—a GMC 6-71 diesel—but I could not see what he was doing to it.

I stepped up close to the stern gunwale. "Ahoy!" I shouted over the wind. "Ahoy there!"

He came around quickly, a box wrench he had been using up-raised in one hand. There were smudges of grease and oil over the front of his sweatshirt, on his hands and arms as well. He owned one of those dark brooding faces, with an aggressive jaw and deep-sunk eyes under heavy brows, that some women seem to find attractive; but now it was pinched-up with annoyance. The cold had turned his lips the color of raw liver: I wondered what he was trying to prove by not wearing a coat of some kind.

He said, "What the hell do you want?"

"Are you Andy Greene?"

"Who wants to know?"

I told him. "Can I come aboard?"

"What for?"

"I'd like to talk to you—"

"I haven't got time to talk now."

"It won't take long."

"I'm busy, friend."

"It's important. I'm here about—"

"Some other time," he said. "Blow away, friend."

Pleasant bastard, aren't you? I thought. I said, "Look, *friend,* all I want is a few minutes of your time—a few answers to some questions about Jerry Carding. Then you can get back to whatever you're doing and I'll be on my way."

Some of the aggressiveness went out of his expression, but not all of it. He got onto his feet, balancing himself on the pitching deck with his feet spread. "The private eye from Frisco, right?" he said.

"That's right."

The deep-sunk eyes studied me; they did not seem very impressed by what they saw. "So what's your interest in the kid?"

"Professional interest. He's part of a case I'm working on."

"What case?"

"You've heard about it. The murders of Jerry's fiance and father."

"They got the guy who killed his old man," Greene said.

"Did they? I'm not so sure."

"Yeah? You think the kid did it?"

"No," I said. "Can I come aboard or not? I don't like shouting this way."

"Waste of time for both of us," he said. "I can't help you, friend. I already told the cops all I know."

"Which is what?"

"Which is nothing. Last time I saw the kid was two weeks ago, when he went out fishing with me. He didn't say a word about going away and I don't have any idea where he went. Okay? Now I got work to do."

He turned away from me and knelt again in front of the Jimmy diesel. I stayed where I was for ten or fifteen seconds, watching him. Irritation was sharp in me—but there was nothing I could do. The boat was his property; if he did not want me aboard, or to do any more talking to me, those were his privileges.

"Maybe I'll see you again, Greene," I said, just to find out if he had anything else to say. But I could have saved my breath. He bent forward, inside the engine compartment, and the only answer I got was the faint clank of the box wrench against metal.

Most of the gray daylight was gone by the time I got back to The Tides; it was almost four thirty. Shadows covered the rolling hills to the east, and the scattered lights up there had a wet glistening look through the fog. Cold rainy night coming up—and there was nothing for me to do now except wait it out and hope that tomorrow turned out to be a more productive day.

In the trunk of my car I keep a small overnight bag for unplanned layovers such as this one. I got it out, carried it into the motel office to register, and then took it up to the room I was given. The cold seemed to have seeped into my bones; my feet felt as if I had been walking barefoot in six inches of snow. So I took a quick shower and afterward made a cup of instant coffee with one of those hot-water dispensers motels put in for guests these days. Then I propped myself up on the bed to do some thinking.

Jerry Carding. He was a central figure, all right. And I was becoming convinced that if I could find him, or discover what had happened to him, I could begin to piece together an explanation for everything.

Go over the facts again, I thought. What did I know and what could I surmise from that knowledge? Well, I knew that he had disappeared sometime after nine o'clock last Sunday night, after leaving the Darden house with a couple of manila envelopes presumably containing an article he'd written. Had he mailed the stamped and addressed envelope? No way of knowing yet. If he had, to whom? Newspaper, maybe, or a news magazine: Jerry had seemed to think the article was important, which meant its subject matter had to be of some news value. But then why hadn't the article surfaced by now, been turned over to the police? Blank. Why had Jerry taken the unaddressed envelope with him? Planning to show it to somebody, possibly—but that seemed inconsistent with the cloak of secrecy he had wrapped around this project of his. Unless—

Blackmail?

No, I didn't like that. From all I had found out about Jerry Carding, a blackmail scheme would be foreign to his nature; what he seemed to care most of all about was establishing a career for himself as an investigative reporter. And if blackmail was what he'd been up to, why take the trouble to write the article at all? Whatever he'd found out, the knowledge alone, would have been enough.

Try it another way, then. Suppose he *had* uncovered something not only newsworthy but damaging to somebody; and suppose this somebody, call him X, found out in turn that Jerry was writing his article and was afraid of public exposure. X could have waylaid him at the post office, before the stamped envelope could be mailed. That would explain Jerry's sudden disappearance—why he failed to ask Kellenbeck for his salary, why he left all his belongings behind—and it would provide a grim probable answer to the question of whether or not he was still alive.

Better theory, that one, but not much better. How could X have known Jerry was on his way to the post office? From watching the Darden house? Farfetched. And if X knew about the article, why wait until Jerry had finished it before going after

118

him? And how could X have found out in the first place, with Jerry being as close-mouthed as he was?

Questions.

And more questions: How could a discovery in Bodega Bay, or an article written about it, tie up with a shooting in San Francisco two days later and a shooting in Brisbane two days after that? Where did the Talbot/Nichols family fit in? Where did Bobbie Reid fit in? What was the significance of the threatening letters and telephone calls to Christine Webster? Why had my office been vandalized? Did the torn corner from the label or decal I had found in Jerry's room mean anything? Did Andy Greene's surly reticence mean anything?

It was like trying to make your way through a labyrinth: you kept moving around, taking this path and that, and all you seemed to find were new and more confusing twists and turns. Unless you figured out the right turns before too much time had passed, or blundered into them, you could become hopelessly lost.

And right now I felt about as lost as you could get.

Hunger pangs drove me out of there at six, down to the Wharf Bar and Restaurant. Where I ate a Crab Louie, drank two bottles of Schlitz, and brooded out at the dark waters of the bay. No rain yet, but the fog had dissipated somewhat and the sky was thick with swollen clouds; the wind made angry moaning sounds and rattled the window glass from time to time. The weather and the nonproductive brooding combined to make me feel frustrated and a little depressed.

I went back to my room and put in a long distance call to Eberhardt's home in San Francisco to see if he had any news. No answer. Out somewhere with his wife for dinner, probably. I tried Dennis Litchak's number; he was in, as he almost always was, and he assured me that everything was fine with my flat. I told him I would be spending the night in Bodega Bay. He told me not to worry, he'd keep on checking until I got home. So much for that.

The first drops of rain began to splatter against the window.

I debated calling Laura Nichols, decided what the hell, she

was paying my wages, and had the motel operator dial her number. It was Karen Nichols who answered. I told her who was calling and asked if her mother was home.

"Yes," she said, "but our lawyer's here and they're having a conference. I suppose I can interrupt them if you want to talk to her."

"That's not necessary. I'm just checking in."

"Where are you? You sound far away."

"In Bodega Bay. Trying to get a line on Jerry Carding."

"Oh. Then you're still investigating?"

"Still at it, yes. But I haven't found out much so far."

"How long will you be there?"

"Until tomorrow sometime. Let me give you the number here, just in case." I did that, and then said, "While I've got you on the phone I'd like to ask you a couple of things."

"What things?"

"Do you or your mother know anyone in Bodega Bay?"

"No."

"Is the name Bobbie Reid familiar to you?"

"Who?"

"Bobbie Reid. R-e-i-d."

"No. Who's she?"

"Someone whose name came up. How about Steve Farmer?"

"No."

"Dave Brodnax?"

"No."

"Lainey Madden?"

"No."

So much for that, too.

I could not think of anyone else to call except Donleavy, and I had already wasted enough long-distance money as it was. So I turned on the TV set and sat staring at it. Opiate of the masses—but not for me, not tonight. I got up again after ten minutes and shut if off.

Sheets of rain now, buffeting the window.

Mournful whistle-and-howl of the wind.

Saturday night, I thought. Not a good night for a man to be

alone, especially not in a storm and place where he has no friends. A night for company, for good conversation, for a warm fire. For a woman. How long since I had last gotten laid? Too damned long. Crusty old bachelor with a beer belly, sloppy habits, and a collection of pulp magazines. No wonder I wasn't getting laid; who would want to climb into the sack with somebody like that? Getting old, too. The last of San Francisco's lone-wolf private eyes . . .

Nuts. San Francisco's only private eye who sits around motel rooms feeling sorry for himself.

I went to the window, stood looking out for awhile and watching rain drool down the glass. Too early to go to bed . . . did I feel like reading? No, but it was better than thinking myself into a blue funk. I took out one of the pulps tucked into the overnight case with the rest of my stuff—a 1940 issue of *Detective Fiction Weekly*—and lay down under the covers with it.

One of the featured novelettes was called "Finger of Doom" and I started to read that first. But I must have been a lot more tired than I'd thought; halfway through the story my eyelids began to feel heavy, my attention wavered and dulled. And I dozed, woke up, tried to read some more, and promptly dropped off for good.

Which had to be one of the few times anybody ever fell asleep reading a story by Cornell Woolrich. . . .

SIXTEEN

I was up at eight o'clock on Sunday morning and in a better frame of mind: ten hours' sleep and a new day. Most of the storm seemed to have blown inland during the night; the rain had slackened to an intermittent drizzle. The overcast was still thick and at a low ceiling, but it did not seem quite as oppressive as it had yesterday afternoon and evening.

When I finished shaving I went out to hunt up breakfast and a Sunday newspaper. No luck. The Wharf Bar and Restaurant was not open this early, nor was anything else in the immediate vicinity. I bought a copy of Saturday's Santa Rosa *Press-Democrat* from a coin-operated machine in Bodega, took it back to the motel, settled for another cup of free instant coffee, and enlightened myself with day-old news.

At ten I gathered my things together and checked out. It was ten-thirty on the nose when I pulled up in front of the Darden house. If nothing else, I was at least punctual.

Mrs. Darden answered my knock and admitted me. She was wearing a tweed suit today, with a blue scarf at the throat, and her graying hair had been neatly brushed for church. Handsome woman, all right. The smile she let me have was warm, as if I were an old friend come to pay a social call.

We went into the parlor, where a girl about eighteen was standing near the fireplace. You could see right away that she was Mrs. Darden's daughter: same short hair, hers being a tawny brown, same attractive features, same hazel eyes, same infectious smile. Besides age, the major differences between them were height and chest development; Sharon was about four inches taller and two bra sizes smaller, which gave her a somewhat willowy look. She was dressed in an ankle-length wool skirt and a bulky knitted sweater.

Her mother introduced us and then excused herself and left the room. Sharon and I sat down. She said, "Mom told me about your talk yesterday. I can't tell you much more about Jerry than she did, I'm afraid."

"This article of Jerry's—he never gave you any clue as to what it was about?"

"No. The only thing he ever said was that it was something which would establish his career as a journalist."

"He seemed positive about that?"

"Oh yes, very positive."

"Can you think of any sort of unusual occurrence in this area recently?" I asked. "Anything that might inspire him?"

"No, there's just nothing. Not much ever happens in Bodega." She said that last sentence not as if she were unhappy about the fact, but as if she were rather proud of it.

Mrs. Darden came back in carrying a tray laden with a porcelain coffee service and a plate of homemade breakfast pastries. She put the tray down on the coffee table, poured a cup for me, and urged that I help myself to the pastries. I did that, not so much to be polite as because I was pretty hungry. And within five seconds, despite using a cake plate and a napkin, I managed

123

to get powdered sugar all over my pants and on the carpet as well. The slob strikes again.

"Oh please, it's all right," Mrs. Darden said when I apologized. There was an almost wistful note in her voice, as though she had once been used to having things spilled on the carpet and was recalling other times it had happened. Maybe her husband had been messy, too; that would explain it.

I put the pastry down for the time being, before I dropped it and the plate too, and sipped some coffee. Then I said to Sharon, "You talked to Jerry before he left last Sunday night?"

"Yes. Only for a minute."

"What did he say?"

"Just that he was going to the post office. I asked him if he had finished his article, if that was what was in the envelopes he had, and he said yes. The only other thing he said was to leave the key out for him."

"Key?"

"To the front door."

"It's our policy not to give out keys to boarders," Mrs. Darden said. "But we do put one under a flower pot on the porch whenever no one is home, or if we know a boarder is going to come in after we're in bed."

I thought that over. "Then you always lock the front door when you retire?"

"Yes."

"What time do you usually go to bed on Sundays?"

"Around eleven."

"And it was after nine when Jerry left?"

"Yes," Sharon said. "Just after."

"About how long would it take him to walk from here to the post office and back again?"

"Well—thirty minutes or so."

"Which indicates he was headed somewhere else besides the post office," I said. "Otherwise he would have expected to be back by ten, when you were both still up, and he wouldn't have asked for the key to be left out. Is there any sort of taxi service in the village?"

124

"No. None."

"Bus service on Sunday night?"

"No."

"So Jerry either planned to walk to where he was going or he was being met by someone." I did some more ruminating. "He was excited, intense, when he left here?"

Sharon nodded.

"Yet he'd just finished writing his article," I said, "and was about to put at least one copy in the mail. And he'd spent all day at the typewriter. He should have been relieved, exhausted—but not still excited. It had to be whatever he was going to do after leaving the post office, or whoever he was going to see, that made him that way."

"But it could still have something to do with the subject of his article, couldn't it?" Mrs. Darden asked. "Even though he'd finished it?"

"Yes. It probably did. How many places in the village are open on Sunday night?"

"Just the tavern. Everything else closes by six."

Sharon said, "Doesn't Mr. Ingles stay open until ten, mom?"

"You're right, I believe he does."

"Mr. Ingles?" I said.

"He owns the Sonoma Cafe. It's on the road just outside the village. You may have noticed it as you drove in."

I hadn't noticed it, but I nodded anyway. And then tackled the pastry again, this time without embarrassing myself, and drank the rest of my coffee. Immediately Mrs. Darden refilled the cup.

I asked, "Do you know where Steve Farmer lives?"

"Across the bay," Sharon said. "On Salmon Creek Road, above the marina."

That was a long walk from Bodega—more than five miles. But if it was Farmer that Jerry had been going to see, for whatever reason, Farmer could have met him here at the post office. Or anybody else could. Or he could have hitchhiked somewhere.

"Do Steve and Jerry get along well?"

"Sure. They're pretty close."

"Did either of them ever speak about a girl named Bobbie Reid?"

"No-o. Is that somebody they know in San Francisco?"

"It's somebody they knew," I said, "and who knew Christine Webster." I did not see any reason to go into detail. "What can you tell me about Gus Kellenbeck?"

"We don't know him very well," Mrs. Darden said. "He only moved here about four years ago, when he bought out what used to be Bay Fishery; and he seldom comes into Bodega. I do know that he's a good businessman. The past couple of years haven't been a boom for anyone in the fishing business—mostly because of poor salmon runs. But he's managed to keep the plant operating at a profit. Or so the talk is. He pays the fishermen top dollar for their catches."

"One of those fishermen being Andy Greene?"

"Yes."

"What's your opinion of Greene?"

"Not very high," Sharon said. "He has a nasty mouth."

"And a nasty disposition," Mrs. Darden added.

"Has he ever been in trouble of any kind?"

"Not that we know about."

"Did Jerry get along with him?"

"I believe so. He never said anything against the man."

"And he also got along with Kellenbeck?"

"Yes. He seemed to."

I tendered a few more questions, without learning anythin else of interest and then finished my second cup of coffee a rose to go. In the foyer both Sharon and her mother wished n luck, and I thanked them for their help, and Mrs. Darden l me out. She seemed almost disappointed to see me leave; h parting smile struck me as even warmer than her welcomi smile. Maybe I reminded her of her husband in more ways tl one. Maybe she found me attractive and desirable and wish she could get to know me better.

Maybe I was an idiot.

Too much libido, that was my problem these days, brough about by too long a period of celibacy. What I ought to do pretty quick, even if I had to pay for it, was get my ashes hauled—as we used to say in the good old days. Otherwise I was going to start salivating every time a woman looked at me with anything except revulsion.

I drove down into the village and parked near the tavern. It was not far from the post office; somebody going in or out could have seen Jerry Carding last Sunday night. Longshot, but it might pay off.

It didn't. The tavern had just opened for business and the bartender on duty only worked until six on Sundays; he did give me the name and address of the night barman, but when I hunted up the place and talked to the guy a few minutes later, he had nothing to tell me. He knew about Jerry's disappearance—it was evidently a major topic of conversation in the Bodega Bay area—but did not know the kid by sight. Last Sunday had been a slow night, he said. Just a few regulars, all of whom had come in early and stayed until around eleven or so. He could not remember anyone arriving or leaving between nine and nine-thirty.

So all right. If Jerry had met someone at the post office and been driven away in a car, I was out of luck; I could not go around knocking on every door within a five-mile radius on the off-chance that someone had been passing by at an opportune moment. Which left me with Mr. Ingles at the Sonoma Cafe. And an even longer longshot: Jerry would have had to leave the village on foot in order to be seen passing the cafe, and Ingles would have had to look out at just the right time in order to see him.

The Sonoma Cafe turned out to be a standard roadside diner—small frame building set back some distance from the highway, facade unadorned by anything except a sign bearing its name. It was open but not doing any business; the lunch counter and a row of brown vinyl booths were deserted. The only person in there was a guy in his sixties, fussing over a pot of something on the stove that had the aroma of fish stew.

He kept on fussing until I sat down at the counter: then he turned and came over to me. He was wearing a white shirt, a bow-tie, and an apron, and he had a shrewd bright-eyed look about him. On his scalp were tufts of hair as thin and fine and colorless as dandelion fluff.

"Afternoon," he said.

"Afternoon. That stew smells good."

"You bet. Like a bowl?"

"Sure." Mrs. Darden's pastry had not done much for my hunger.

He ladled some into a bowl, put the bowl and a couple of packets of crackers on a plate. When he set the food in front of me I said, "Would your name be Ingles?"

"It would. How'd you know?"

"Mrs. Darden mentioned that you owned this place." I went on to tell him who I was and what I was doing in Bodega.

He looked more than a little interested: the village-gossip type, I thought. He leaned on the counter and studied me with his shrewd eyes. "Read about you in the papers," he said. "Private eye, eh? Never met a private eye before. Don't look nothing like Jim Garner, do you?"

"Jim Garner?"

" 'The Rockford Files.' Mean you don't watch that show on TV?"

"No."

"Ought to. Got lots of action, lots of cars getting smashed up."

"Uh-huh." I tasted the stew. A little salty but otherwise not bad. "Do you know Jerry Carding, Mr. Ingles?"

"Sure do. Used to eat in here once in a while. Damned funny the way he disappeared; damned funny. Got the whole town buzzing."

"I was hoping you might have seen him last Sunday night. Say between nine and ten?"

"Nosir," he said immediately. "I'd of remembered it if I had. How come you're asking me? Police didn't come around when they was here." He sounded disappointed that they hadn't.

"This is one of the few places open on Sunday nights," I said. "And there's a chance he left the village on foot. Is it possible one of your customers saw him?"

"One of my customers? Well now." Ingles scratched his scalp and seemed to do some memory cudgeling. "Zach Judson, maybe."

"Oh?"

"Zach stopped in for a cup of coffee around nine, as I recall. On his way home from some lodge doings in Tomales. Stayed about a half hour. Could be he saw the boy; ain't talked to him since."

"Does Judson live in Bodega?"

"Nope. Jenner."

Jenner was a tiny place about fifteen miles up the coast. I said, "Could you give me his telephone number?"

"Nosir."

"Pardon?"

"I said nosir, I won't give you his number."

"Why not?"

"Because he don't have a telephone," Ingles said, and cackled at his own humor. "Old Zach's deaf as a post in one ear and half-deaf in the other. Wouldn't hear a phone ringing if he was sitting on it."

"You *can* give me his address, can't you?"

"Sure. Cost you a buck, though." He winked at me. "Service charge."

A buck. And a thirty-mile round trip to Jenner that would probably turn out to be a waste of time; for all I knew Judson could be in Tomales again for more lodge doings, and it was doubtful that he had seen Jerry Carding anyway. But what else did I have to do? Hunt up Steve Farmer and try to pump him again about Bobbie Reid? That was about it—and it struck me as a last resort, the thing to do before tossing in the towel and heading home to San Francisco.

I sighed and got my wallet out and put a dollar bill on the counter. Ingles made it disappear in two seconds flat, as if he was afraid I might change my mind. Then he grinned at me and said, "Zach's is the last house on the west side of the highway, just before you get into Jenner. Big old gingerbready place, looks like it'd fall down if a good wind come along."

"Thanks." I finished my stew, gave him some more money for that, and slid a dime tip under the plate when he wasn't looking. The stew had not been all that good and neither had he.

As I started out he called after me, "Tune in 'The Rockford Files' one of these nights. That Jim Garner's a real good detective."

Me too, I thought wryly. Even if I don't have my own TV show.

I headed the car north on Highway 1. The winding two-lane road had little traffic for a Sunday afternoon, but the fog had come back again, heavy and wet, and it made the pavement slick and visibility poor; it was forty-five minutes before I crossed the bridge spanning the Russian River and approached Jenner.

The hamlet—what there was of it—was located at the mouth of the river, where it widened out and joined the ocean. To the west, between the road and the water, were a lot of tide flats and a few houses. The last house south of Jenner matched Ingles' description: a ramshackle twenties-style structure that seemed to list inland, as if the constant wind off the sea had been too much for it. A lone cypress tree grew in the muddy front yard, wind-bent and leaning companionably in the same direction; parked near it was a 1940s vintage Chevvy pick-up. Lights glowed behind chintz curtains in one front window.

I took my car into the yard and put it next to the pick-up. When I got out a fat lazy-looking dog came around from behind the house, barked once in an indifferent way, and then waddled off again. I climbed sagging steps onto the front porch and rapped on the door.

Nobody answered. Ingles had said Zach Judson was all but deaf, I remembered; I tried again, using my fist this time, pounding hard enough to rattle the wood in its frame. That got results. The door creaked open pretty soon and a guy about seventy peered out at me through wire-framed spectacles. He had a gnarly face, a mop of unkempt white hair, and one of those big old-fashioned plastic hearing aids hooked over one ear.

He said, "Yep?" in a tone that wondered if I was going to try to sell him something.

"Mr. Judson?"

"Yep?"

I told him my name. "I'm a detective, and I—"

"You say detective?"

"Yes, sir. Investigating the disappearance of Jerry Carding."

"Who?"

"Jerry Carding."

"Never heard of any Jerry Carling."

"Carding, Mr. Judson. Jerry *Carding*."

"Never heard of any Jerry Carding."

"The story's been in all the papers and on TV—"

"Don't read the papers. Don't own a TV."

"He vanished from Bodega last Sunday night, between nine and ten o'clock," I said. "A young fellow about twenty, dark hair, Fu Manchu mustache. I understand you were in Bodega around that time and I thought you might have seen him."

"Yep," Judson said.

"Sir?"

"Yep. Did see him."

Well now. "Where was this, Mr. Judson?"

"On the highway. Near Ingles' cafe."

"Was he alone?"

"Yep. Hitchhiking."

"He thumbed you, then?"

"Yep."

"But you didn't stop for him?"

"*Did* stop for him. Used to hitch rides myself, back when. Decent young fella. Polite, good manners. Missing, you say?"

"Yes." There was a tenseness inside me now; this was the kind of break I had been looking for. "You took him where, Mr. Judson?"

"What?"

"Where did you take him?"

"Not far. Just up the road a ways."

"How far up the road?"

"To the Kellenbeck Fish Company," he said.

SEVENTEEN

I did some hard thinking on the way back to Bodega Bay.

Jerry Carding had hitchhiked to the Kellenbeck Fish Company last Sunday night. All right. Zach Judson had not seen him approach the plant, but it was a safe assumption that it had been Jerry's destination; there was nothing else in the vicinity, no other businesses or private homes. Meeting someone there? Could be. But then why not meet in Bodega instead? As it was, Jerry had had to walk partway and hitch a ride the rest of the way.

The other possibility was that he had gone to the fish company to look for something, either inside the building or somewhere around it. Something connected with the article he'd written; that seemed likely. Ten o'clock on a Sunday night—a nocturnal prowl. It was the kind of thing an adventurous kid, a kid who wanted to be an investigative reporter, might do.

But what had happened then? Had Jerry completed his search, with or without finding what he'd come after, and later hitchhiked away from Bodega Bay? Or had somebody found him there and been responsible for his disappearance?

And the big question—why? What was there about the Kellenbeck Fish Company that would inspire a "career-making" article and a secret late-evening visit? Yes, and why go there *after* he had finished the article?

I focused my thoughts on Gus Kellenbeck. According to Mrs. Darden, the past couple of years had not been a boon for anyone in the fishing business; yet Kellenbeck had managed to keep his plant operating at a profit. It was possible that he was mixed up in some sort of illegal enterprise, such as price-fixing or substituting and selling one kind of processed fish for another. But that sort of thing had little news value; it happened all the time, in one form or another. Even a novice like Jerry would have known that.

What *else* could it be?

What else . . .

There was an itching sensation at the back of my mind, the kind I seem always to have when there's something caught and trying to struggle out of my subconscious. Something significant I had seen or heard. It gave me a vague feeling of excitement, as if I were poised on the edge of breakthrough knowledge: remember what it was, take that one right turn, and I would be on my way into all the other right turns that led out of the labyrinth.

Only it would not come, not yet; the harder I tried to get hold of it, the tighter it seemed to wedge back. Let it alone, then. It would pop through sooner or later, the way nagging bits of information you can't quite remember—names, dates, titles of books or movies—come popping through once you stop thinking about them.

It was four-thirty and just starting to get dark when I neared the Kellenbeck Fish Company. On impulse I swung the car onto the deserted gravel area in front. The building had a dark abandoned look in the fog and the late-afternoon gloom; closed on

Sundays, I thought, nobody here. But I got out anyway and went around onto the rear dock.

The corrugated iron doors were closed and padlocked; I could see that without going over there. Instead I wandered to the foot of the rickety pier. There was nothing on it, no boats tied up at its end. Beyond, the gray water was scummed with mist. And on the opposite shore, Bodega Head was just a lumpish outline dotted here and there with ghostly lights from the houses above the marina.

I turned to look at the building again. The itching sensation came back, but with the same nonresults. Maybe if I had another talk with Kellenbeck, I thought; maybe that would help me remember. At the least I could see how he reacted when I mentioned Jerry Carding's visit here last Sunday evening.

So I returned to the car and drove to The Tides and hunted up a public telephone. There was a listing for Kellenbeck in the Sonoma County directory with an address in Carmet-by-the-Sea. Carmet was an older development of homes a few miles back to the north, right on the ocean; I had passed by it twice on the trip to and from Jenner.

I got there inside of twenty minutes, but it was another ten before I located Kellenbeck's place; the homes were well spread out along the east side of the highway and the fog made it difficult to read the street signs. The house turned out to be a big knotty-pine A-frame with a lot of glass facing out toward the Pacific. Even for Carmet, where homes would not come cheap because of the view, it looked to be worth a pretty good chunk of money. Kellenbeck was doing well for himself, all right—maybe too well for the owner of a minor fish-processing plant. You did not buy or build a house like this with just a small-businessman's profits.

The trip here seemed to be a wasted effort, though. All the windows were dark, and so were those in the adjacent garage. Just to be sure I went up onto the porch and rang the bell. No answer.

A pair of mist-smeared headlights poked toward me as I was coming back to the car. Kellenbeck? But it wasn't; the headlights belonged to a low-slung sports job, not the Cadillac I had seen yesterday at the fish company, and it drifted on by.

I got into the car and sat there and tried to decide what to do next. Take another room for the night at The Tides Motel and then brace Kellenbeck tomorrow—that seemed like the best idea. The other alternative, hanging around here and hoping that he *did* show up before long, had no appeal. For all I knew he was out somewhere for the evening, visiting friends or indulging his fondness for liquor; and I had no idea where to go looking for him—

The itching again.

Then, all at once, I remembered.

It came out of my subconscious clear and sharp—something I had seen, something odd—and right on its heels was another fragment. I put on the dome light, took out the torn corner I had found in Jerry Carding's room at the Darden house, and looked at it. Then I began to construct a mental blueprint, testing it with some of the questions I had asked myself and other people the past few days. And I remembered something else then, one more fragment. And sketched in a few more connecting lines.

And there it was.

Not a complete blueprint; it didn't explain all the twists and turns, did not show me all the way to the end. But the things it did show made sense: What it was Jerry had found out, the subject of his article. Why he might have gone to the fish company last Sunday night. Why he had disappeared.

Why his father had been murdered in Brisbane on Thursday.

Yet I had no proof of any of it. It was speculation, personal observation—just like my account of what had happened when Martin Talbot discovered Victor Carding's body. Eberhardt and Donleavy would want to check it out if I took it to them cold, and so would the Federal authorities; but no search warrants could be obtained without some sort of evidential cause, and if Kellenbeck was alerted there might not *be* any evidence left to find. He could take steps to cover himself, bluff through even a Federal investigation, get off scot-free.

I *had* to have proof, damn it. Something solid to back up my theories. And I knew where I might be able to find it. . . .

No, I thought then. Uh-uh. You don't break laws, remember? Or go skulking around in the night like the pulp private eyes. You want to get your license revoked?

You want a murderer to maybe go unpunished?

Call up Eberhardt. Lay it in his lap.

Not without proof. You could *try* to get it; go there, see how things look. At least make the effort.

I spent another couple of minutes arguing with myself. But it was no contest: I started the car and went away to skulk in the night.

The Kellenbeck Fish Company was still dark and so wrapped in fog now that it had a two-dimensional look, like a shape cut from heavy black paper. I drove on past it by a hundred yards, parked off the road alongside a jumble of shoreline rocks. From under the dash I unclipped the flashlight I keep there and dropped it into my coat pocket. Blurred yellow headlight beams brightened the road behind me; I waited until the car hissed past and disappeared into the mist before I got out and hurried back toward the building.

The night had an eerie muffled stillness, marred only by the ringing of fog bells out on the channel buoys and the faint lapping of the bay water against the pilings; the crunch of my footfalls seemed unnaturally loud as I crossed the gravel parking area. When I got to the shedlike enclosure I paused in the shadows to test the door there. Locked—and so secure in its frame that it did not rattle when I tugged on the knob. If I was going to get in at all, it would have to be at the rear.

I crossed to the catwalk. It was pitch-black along there; I stayed in close to the building wall, feeling my way along it until I came out onto the dock. The writhing fog created vague spectral shadows among the stacks of crab pots, brushed my face with a spidery wetness. Visibility was no more than two hundred yards. Even the lights on Bodega Head were swaddled, hidden inside the fogbanks.

The padlock on the corrugated doors was an old Yale with a heavy base and a thick steel loop. You would need a hacksaw and an hour's work to cut through it, and I was not about to try such shenanigans anyway. I felt nervous enough as it was. Cold sweat had formed under my arms, the palms of my hands were damp, sticky. Maybe the pulp detectives were good at this sort of thing; maybe Jim Garner was on "The Rockford Files." Not me.

I moved to the far side of the doors. In the wall there, near where the crab pots were, was a window made opaque by an accumulation of grime. When I stepped up close to it I could see it was the kind with two sashes, one overlapping the other vertically. I put the heel of my hand against the frame of the lower piece and shoved upward. Latched at the middle but not at the bottom. And a loose latch at that because it rose a quarter of an inch before binding with a creaky sound. It could probably be forced without too much trouble.

Which brought me to the moment of reckoning. The only way I was going to get inside was through this window; so I either forced it or gave the whole idea up. All I was guilty of so far was trespassing. But if I forced the window it was felony breaking-and-entering—a crime that would cost me my license and maybe put me in prison if anybody found out about it.

If anybody found out, I thought. Who was going to find out? If I discovered what I expected to, I could tell Eberhardt I came by it in a legal fashion. A little white lie. And Kellenbeck's arrest and conviction for murder would go a long way toward appeasing my conscience.

I wiped moisture off my face, hunched my shoulders against the wind blowing in across the water, and laid both hands on the sash frame. Bent my knees and heaved upward. The lock creaked again; the window pane rattled. I dipped lower, locked my elbows, heaved a second time. A third. A fourth—

There was a loud groaning noise, then a sudden snapping, and the sash wobbled upward.

138

The noise made me jerk my head around and look furtively around the empty dock. A seagull screeched somewhere in the fog—a cry that sounded almost mocking. I took a couple of deep breaths; my heart was pounding as if I had just run the quarter-mile. Then I eased the sash up as far as it would go, swung my leg over the sill. And ducked under and up into blackness heavy with the odors of fish and brine.

With my back to the window, I got the flashlight out, shielded the lens with my hand, and switched it on. Shellfish tanks, a massive refrigeration unit that gave off palpable waves of cold. Beyond, where Kellenbeck's office was, the bank of machinery and conveyor belts formed a mass of shadowy outlines.

I shuffled away from the window and around the nearest of the tanks, holding the flash pointed downward at thigh level. The light glistened over the fish scales speckling the floor, picked out a stack of crates just in time to keep me from plowing into them. My mouth was dry; I worked saliva through it as I stepped off to the left, lifted the flash and unshielded it long enough to make a single horizontal sweep. Open floor past the crates, except for the machinery and four big weighing scales set side by side like a row of deactivated robots. In the gloom ahead there was a dullish reflection of the beam: the window in the office cubicle.

Following the light, I made my way over there. The closer I got to it, the more hushed the warehouse became; I could no longer hear even the muffled ringing of the fog bells. The scraping of my shoes on the slick floor was the only sound.

The door to the office was closed. Locked? No, it opened silently when I rotated the knob. I stepped inside, leaving the door open, and let the light flicker over Kellenbeck's desk. Same clutter of papers and junk that I had seen yesterday. Except for one thing. And I found that right away, in the bottom desk drawer where I had watched Kellenbeck put it.

The bottle of Canadian whiskey.

The evidence.

I hauled it out by its cap so I would not smear any clear fingerprints on the glass. Shined the flash on it. The label carried the name of a popular brand and was brown with a black-lined square around the edges—the same colors, the same pattern, that was on the torn corner from Jerry Carding's room. Which was part of what I had remembered earlier. The first thing, the one that had been itching at the back of my mind, was the way Kellenbeck had kept looking at the bottle while I was talking to him, the way he had caught it up so quickly by its bare neck and put it away inside the drawer. I had already seen him drinking from it during business hours; why hide it unless there was something about it he did not want me to notice. Something I *had* noticed, but without realizing it at the time.

The bare neck: it had no tax stamp.

And the label would be counterfeit.

Bootleg liquor.

That was where Kellenbeck's profits were coming from and that was what Jerry Carding had found out: Kellenbeck was an illicit-whiskey distributor.

Most people think of bootlegging as something that went out with Prohibition; but the fact is, it's still a multimillion dollar business in the United States. And not just in the South. It goes on along the West Coast too, just as it used to in the days of the Volstead Act when ships outfitted as distilleries—big stills in their holds, bottling equipment, labels for a dozen different kinds of Canadian whiskey—were brought down from Canada and anchored twenty-five miles offshore. Nowadays the stuff was probably made at some isolated spot across the border and carried down the coast by freighter or large fishing boat. But it would still be handled in pretty much the same way: picked up by small craft, stored somewhere nearby until it could be trucked out to customers throughout the state.

Kellenbeck's big mistake was committing murder to keep his activities a secret; his little mistake was drinking his own hooch instead of the genuine stuff. Maybe he liked it because it packed a heftier wallop. Yeah, well, it was going to help wallop him right into San Quentin.

I made a hurried check through the rest of the desk and through the papers on top of it. Everything seemed to pertain

140

to the fish company operations, as did everything in the single file cabinet. But I did find two more bottles of bootleg tucked away inside a small storage closet. On impulse I took one of them and wedged it out of sight behind the file cabinet. Just in case the bottle missing from his desk made Kellenbeck suspicious and he decided to get rid of the rest of it. In a sense I was tampering with evidence, but that was a technicality and the hell with it; I was in pretty deep as it was. And it would insure that the Justice Department investigators found something incriminating when they showed up with search warrants.

Time for me to get out of here, I thought. Past time: I had been in the building for half an hour—I was more nervous than ever now, and sweating like the proverbial pig. I caught up the desk bottle, swept the flash over the office once more: everything looked as I had found it. Then I went out, closed the door behind me, shielded the flash beam again and trailed it back across the warehouse.

When I reached the window the cold air from the refrigeration unit and the icy wind blowing in from outside made me shiver. I hunched my shoulders, switched off the flash. Out on the dock fog swirled around the crab pots, giving them an insubstantial, surreal look in the darkness. Quickly I lifted one leg over the sill, straddled it, and started to swing out.

Movement behind the nearest of the crab pots.

A board creaked.

Somebody there—

Blinding white light errupted out of the mist, pinned me, made me recoil and crack the back of my head against the window sash.

"Stay where you are, asshole," a harsh voice said behind the glare. "I've got a gun; I'll blow you away if you move."

But it was not Gus Kellenbeck.

The voice belonged to Andy Greene.

EIGHTEEN

I stayed frozen, half in and half out of the window, the damned bottle in my right hand and hanging out where Greene could see it. Fear climbed up into my throat and lodged there like a glob of bitter mucus. The light burned against my eyes; I squeezed the lids down to slits.

"All right," he said. "Let go the bottle."

"Listen, Greene—"

"Now, goddamn it!"

I released the bottle, heard it clatter on the dock and roll back in against the wall. At the same time I turned my head a little so I was no longer looking directly into the glare. Tendrils of fog curled through the beam, capered at its edges like will-o'-the-wisps. And gave Greene, behind it, a dark ectoplasmic look, as if he were something only half-materialized. The wet touch of the mist against my face made my skin crawl.

"Back inside," Greene said. "Nice and slow. Then turn around and walk away from the window."

The muscles in my arms and legs were cramped with tension; the joints did not seem to want to bend, so that when I forced myself back off the sill it was in awkward, mannequin-stiff movements. The jet of light dipped lower, came forward through the opening. I pivoted away from it, blinking, licking at the gunmetal taste in my mouth. And then began to pace toward the shellfish tanks.

Behind me Greene made scraping sounds as he climbed through the window. The skin on my back was still crawling; it was bad enough to face a man with a gun, even when you couldn't see him, but to have him behind you in the dark was twice as unnerving.

When I reached the first of the tanks, ten paces away, Greene's voice said, "That's far enough." I stopped, made a careful three-quarters turn back toward him. He was moving laterally to his left, along the inner wall; the flash beam stayed centered on me, flickering a little with his movements. Then he came to a standstill, and seconds later there were a series of faint clicks. The darkness shrank into random pockets of shadow as high-wattage bulbs strung along the rafters winked on.

I did some more blinking. Greene shut off a big four-cell flashlight, jammed it into the pocket of a blue pea jacket; then he motioned me over toward the locked entrance doors, where there was nothing for me to get my hands on, and halved the distance between us when I got there. His face was expressionless. But the deep-sunk eyes looked as cold and flat and deadly as the Browning 9 mm automatic in his right hand.

Looking at him, I felt swirls of black rage under the fear. Rage at him, at Kellenbeck, at what had been done to Jerry Carding and his father. And rage at myself for coming here like a damned fool, breaking the law, getting caught up this way. Stupid. *Stupid*.

We stood watching each other for eight or ten seconds. Then I said, "What happens now, Greene?" My voice had sounded cracked when I started to speak at the window, but these words came out in the same hard monotone he had been using.

"What do you think happens?"

"You call up Kellenbeck. He calls up the county police and has me arrested for breaking-and-entering."

Greene showed me his teeth. "You'd like that, wouldn't you," he said.

"Why should I like it?"

"Go ahead, play dumb if you want. But you don't bluff your way out of this."

"Neither do you," I said. "Not any more."

"What the hell does that mean?"

"It means I'm not the only one who's onto you."

"Bullshit. Cops knew anything, *they'd* be here, not you."

"They'll be here before long. Count on it."

"Not tonight. Not while you're still around—"

There was a sudden banging sound in the front part of the building, where the tacked-on shed was. Greene tensed. I half-turned, looking up toward a closed door adjacent to the bank of machinery—but the glimmer of hope inside me died in the next second when the door opened and Gus Kellenbeck came shambling through.

"Andy? I saw the lights, I—" He quit talking and pulled up short, gaping at me and at the gun in Greene's hand. His eyes had a glassy look and there was a slackness to his mouth; he seemed to sway a little. "Jesus, Andy," he said in a different voice. "Jesus."

I moved sideways a couple of steps, carefully, so I could see both of them without swiveling my head back and forth. The Browning moved with me.

When Greene looked at Kellenbeck again his upper lip flattened in against his teeth. "You goddamn drunk," he said, and that told me all I needed to know about how things stood between the two of them. Maybe the bootlegging had been Kellenbeck's scam in the beginning, and he had brought Greene in for the use of his boat; but whether or not that was it, Greene was the one running the show now.

144

"I only had a few," Kellenbeck said, "I lost track of the time."
He slid a hand across gray-stubbled cheeks, across his slacked
mouth. "What's *he* doing here, Andy? Why'd you bring him
here?"

"I didn't bring him here. I saw him snooping around your
house and decided to follow him, see what he was up to. Good
thing I did. He came straight here, busted in, and searched your
office; I nailed him on the way out."

Damned *fool*, I thought again. It must have been Greene in
that low-slung sports job in Carmet. And him again in the car
that passed after I parked down the highway; I had been too
intent on getting into the building, on playing the souped-up
detective, to notice it was the same car both times.

"He knows, then," Kellenbeck said. He sounded sick and
frightened.

"Sure he knows. What's the matter with you?"

"How did he find out?"

"How do you think? You and that fucking hooch. I told you
not to keep any of it around."

Kellenbeck moved forward a couple of steps. A belch came
out of him; he wiped his mouth again. "Andy," he said,
"Andy . . "

"Shut up."

"Let him say it, Greene," I said. The rage was stronger,
blacker, inside me now—and that was good because it smothered
the fear. Blood made a surflike pounding in my temples.

"You shut up too."

I looked at Kellenbeck. "He's planning to kill me, all right
Is that what you want? Another murder on your conscience?"

"Andy, for Christ's sake. . . ."

"Killing me won't get you off the hook," I said. "What do
you think will happen if I disappear like Jerry Carding—two
disappearances within a week? The cops will be all over this
place. And they'll find out, Kellenbeck, just like I did—"

"One more word," Greene said, "I'll blow you away right
now."

He meant it; I could hear it in his voice and see it in his

eyes when I faced him. I locked my teeth together, made myself stand still. Made myself not think about dying, because if I did the rage and the thin edge of panic would prod me into doing something crazy, like trying to jump him for the gun.

"He's right, Andy," Kellenbeck said. His face had a collapsing look, as if all the muscles had loosened at once. "You know he is."

"The hell he's right. We can cover this one too."

"How?"

"Get rid of any more hooch you've got stashed, stay out of touch with the people up north. Let the cops come around; there won't be anything for them to find."

"But suppose he's told somebody something?"

"He hasn't told anybody anything. He's just a smart-guy private dick, that's all. Working on his own."

"I don't know, Andy. Another killing . . . I don't know if I can handle it, face the cops again, all those questions. . . . "

"Sure you can, Gus. You'll be fine, baby."

There was something in the way Green said that, something in his voice that jarred an insight into my mind. Kellenbeck was a drunk and he was coming apart; it was a good bet he would let something slip to the police, maybe even blurt out a confession, when the pressure got too heavy. And Greene knew that as well as I did.

He was planning to kill Kellenbeck too.

I wanted to say something to Kellenbeck, try to turn him against Greene. But I knew if I did that, Greene would use the gun on me without hesitation. He was in total command; there was nothing I could do and nothing Kellenbeck could do.

Not yet, I told myself. Not *yet*.

Kellenbeck belched again, sickly. "Okay," he said. "I guess we got no choice. But Jesus, let's get it over with."

"Your car right out front?"

"Yeah."

"You sober enough to drive?"

146

"Yeah."

"Head out, then. Get the car started."

Kellenbeck nodded, put his back to us, and went into the shed with uneven jerky strides. When the outer door banged a few seconds later Greene said to me, "Your turn. Move."

I moved. The joints in my legs still felt stiff and there was a tight prickling sensation in my groin. I had an impulse to grab hold of the door on my way through, try to slam it shut between us; but it was standing too wide, and Greene had crowded up close behind me. The shed was full of boxes, tools, machine parts—none of them within reaching distance. I opened the outer door, kept my hand on the knob for a second. Greene jabbed me with the automatic. And I let go, struggling with my control, and went out into the cold darkness.

Fog crawled over the highway, obscured all but a three-hundred-yard strip of it. No headlights showed anywhere in the mist. Kellenbeck's Cadillac was slewed in near one of the hoists a few feet away; the engine was running and the lights were on. Greene told me to get into the back seat, slide over against the far door—and waited until I did that before he got in with me, holding the Browning in close to his body so there was no chance of me making a lunge for it.

"Okay," he said to Kellenbeck. "You know where."

Nothing from Kellenbeck. His breathing was rapid and irregular; I could smell the sour whiskey fumes even from where I was. The shape he was in, I thought he might kick the accelerator hard enough to buck the car and throw Greene off-balance. I braced my feet and body, tensing. But Greene anticipated that too; he issued a sharp warning to take it easy, drive slow. And Kellenbeck, obeying, crawled the damned car out of the lot and onto the highway, northbound.

I sat with my hands fisted on my knees, watching Greene in the faint glow of the dashlights. He was sitting half-turned toward me and he still had the gun pulled in against his chest. I thought: God, if I could get my hands on him I'd tear him in half. I thought: I'm being taken for a ride, private eye being taken for a goddamn ride just like in the pulps. I thought: Is

147

this how Jerry Carding felt—twenty-year-old kid, scared, shaking, on his way to die?

Wild thoughts. Breeding more wild impulses. The rage and the fear boiling inside me now like gases coming to an explosion point. I had to do something to keep the lid on my control; if I didn't, if I gave in to the impulses—

I said, "Where are we going? Your boat, Greene, is that it? A little trip out into the ocean?" Talking was the answer. Making words to keep from making myself dead. "Sure. The deep-six. Take me out a mile or two, shoot me or knock me out, weight my body, and I'm gone without a trace. Just like Jerry Carding."

Greene had nothing to say.

"Let's see if I can put it together," I said. "How did Jerry find out about the bootlegging? Overheard the two of you talking, maybe, when you didn't know he was around. Sure, that makes sense. So he does a little investigating, gets hold of a bottle of hooch or the label off of one. But instead of going to the police right away he decides to write an article first; that way, when the story breaks, he can have it published immediately. He'll not only be a full-fledged hero, he'll be an overnight sensation as a journalist.

"He finishes the article on Sunday night, takes the original and his only carbon down to the post office. But he doesn't mail both of them. Just the carbon, to somebody for safe-keeping; the original he keeps with him. Then he heads straight for the—"

"Shut up," Kellenbeck said. "Andy, tell him to shut the hell up. I don't want to listen to this."

Greene said, "Let him talk. The hell with it."

"Then Jerry heads straight for the fish company," I said. "Why? Because he's found out Sunday is the night you take the boat out to pick up a load of whiskey—not every Sunday but once or twice a month, say—and he's also found out you leave from the warehouse when you do go, sometime after ten o'clock. If you're heading out that night he'll call in the Coast Guard and have them waiting when you get back; and he'll also have the original of his article ready to turn over to one of the San Francisco papers. If you're not going out, he'll carry the article back to his room and wait another week or however long it takes until you do.

"When he gets to the fish company he hides somewhere to watch and wait. And the two of you show up. Then something happens—maybe he makes a noise, maybe he's not hidden as well as he thinks—and you grab him. You find the article, you read it, you know he's onto you. It's the kid's death warrant."

We had reached the north rim of the bay. Ahead, through the windshield and through swirls of fog, I could see the turnoff for the road that looped around to Bodega Head.

"But first you've got to know if there are any other copies of that article. You force him to tell you about the carbon, who he mailed it to, and it turns out to be his father down in Brisbane. You can't get the carbon out of the post office; you've got to wait until it's delivered. So the next day you go down to Brisbane and watch Victor Carding's mailbox until the mail is delivered and then check for the carbon.

"Only it doesn't show up on Monday, or on Tuesday or Wednesday either; the mail service being what it is, the envelope isn't delivered until Thursday. But Carding gets to the box before you can, maybe because he's looking for some word from his son. He picks up the mail—the article and a couple of bills—and opens Jerry's envelope right away and starts to read. That leaves you no choice. You brace him with the .38 you were carrying then, take him into the garage, and shoot him. Then you put the gun in his hand—make it look like suicide, keep the police from doing too much digging."

Kellenbeck had made the turn and we were starting around toward the marina. I could just make out the ghost shapes of masts and hulls through gaps in the fog screen.

"But even if Martin Talbot hadn't arrived a few minutes later to screw things up, it wouldn't have worked. No nitrate traces on Carding's hands or powder marks on his clothes: he couldn't have shot himself. The police would still have known it was murder.

"You see how it is, Greene? It's the little things people like you always overlook, the little things that trip you up. It'll be some other little thing, or a combination of them, that finally puts your ass in the gas chamber."

That got a small noise out of Kellenbeck. Greene said, "Smart guy. You like to listen to yourself trying to be smart? Go on, talk some more. Talk all you want while you still can."

But I was through talking. And through teetering on the brink of panic. The wildness was gone; I had talked myself calm, gotten a lock again on emotions and impulses. Intellect was going to get me out of this if anything was. If I panicked, there was no way out: I was a dead man for sure.

We had drawn abreast of the marina now. Vague shimmers of light marked the location of houses along the Head, but there were no lights among the boats—just pale night bulbs scattered above the ramp and the floating walkways. The road, as it had been all the way over from the main highway, was a wet empty stripe in the darkness.

Kellenbeck eased the Cadillac onto the shoulder opposite the ramp. Greene got out first, waited for Kellenbeck, and then motioned me across the seat. There was more wind here and it stung my cheeks with icy wetness; the air was painfully cold in my lungs. I glanced down the road, up at the outlines of the nearest house, over at the boat slips. Nothing stirred anywhere. No help anywhere.

We went across the road and up onto the ramp, Kellenbeck in front of me and Greene behind me by six paces. Sounds drifted out of the fog: the creak of caulked joints and rigging, the thud of a hull against a board float, the buoy bells. I kept moving my head in quadrants, looking for something, anything, to give me an opening, a chance for escape. Fog, wind, empty boats, black water—nothing.

At the end of the ramp Kellenbeck went down the short metal ladder without turning; I heard the thump he made as he dropped off onto the nearest float. When I got to the ladder I turned to face Greene. But he had halted too, and there were still six or seven feet between us—too far for me to even think about making a play for the gun. He waited until I descended the ladder before he approached it, and then it was at an angle so that I had no way of lunging up at him between the handrails. There was nothing I could do except leave the ladder and sidestep along the swaying float. Watch him come down only when I got far enough away to suit him.

Kellenbeck was already on board the *Kingfisher*, standing with his back to the wheelhouse. The water was choppy enough to rock the troller; he had his feet spread wide and one hand up at his mouth, as if the motion had combined with the alcohol in his system to make him nauseous. I came up abaft, hesitated again. Greene slowed and made an impatient slicing gesture with the gun. Kellenbeck reacted as though it was meant for him too: He turned as I climbed over the gunwale and groped his way inside the wheelhouse.

I backed over there, adjusting my balance to the deck roll. Greene swung aboard. Binnacle lights went on inside, one of them a chart lamp that cut away most of the blackness. The wheelhouse, I saw as I stepped through the entrance way, was about ten feet square and empty except for operating equipment and a pair of wooden storage lockers; the bulkheads were all bare. On the port side was a narrow companionway that would lead belowdecks to Greene's sleeping quarters.

I moved to the starboard bulkhead and put my back to it. Kellenbeck was next to the wheel; the glow from the lights gave his face a surreal cast. Greene stood framed in the entrance way, his left shoulder braced at its edge, the gun cocked toward me at his right hip.

"What the hell're you waiting for?" he said to Kellenbeck. "Start the engine. You know where the keys are."

Kellenbeck's throat seemed to be working spasmodically. "I don't feel so good, Andy. You got any liquor on board?"

"No."

"You sure? Christ, I need a drink bad."

"I said no. I want you sober; it'll be tricky enough following the channel in this fog. Now get to it."

In shaky movements Kellenbeck fumbled under the binnacle,

came up with a set of keys, and spent fifteen seconds fitting one into the ignition and firing the diesel. The powerful engine made a guttural throbbing noise, like the magnified purr of a cat, and I could feel the vibrations beneath my feet.

Greene stepped inside and one pace to his right, toward me. "Cast off the lines, Gus."

I watched Kellenbeck walk around behind him and disappear astern. My nerves were beginning to jangle again; the panic simmered just below the surface of my thoughts. Time was running out. Once we were out into the bay, my chances would be twice as slim as they were now—and once we passed break-water at the Bodega Head jetty, into open sea, they would be all but nonexistent. Now was the time to make my move, while I was alone here with Greene. Except that I had no move to make. Maybe I would have to jump him sooner or later, but I could not bring myself to do it yet. It was the last thing to do, the last move, because in close quarters like these I knew it would probably be the last move I would ever make.

Two or three long minutes passed before Kellenbeck came back. One hand was hovering at his mouth again; he looked even sicker than before. When he took the wheel Greene backed over to the entrance way, braced himself the way he had earlier.

Kellenbeck put on the running lights, the windshield wipers, an outside spotlight that sliced a thin diffused beam into the mist. He worked the throttle and we began to creep forward out of the slip, into the narrow marina channel. Wind-swells increased the roll-and-sway of the boat; I put my hands flat against the bulkhead and widened my stance. At the wheel Kellenbeck began to make a series of liquidy gagging sounds that were audible even above the diesel pulse.

Through the windshield, fog churned and appeared to hurl itself in gray streaks against the glass. I could see patches of black water but nothing else: It seemed we were out of the marina now and into the bay.

Kellenbeck was still gagging.

The boat rolled left, pitched right, rolled left.

And Kellenbeck let go of the wheel, lurched around, said,

"Andy, Jesus, take over, I got to puke." And clamped both hands to his mouth and came staggering toward the entrance way.

Right between Greene and me.

My reaction was instinctive and immediate, without thought of any kind. I lunged off the bulkhead and into Kellenbeck, caught hold of his jacket to keep him in front of me—Greene yelled something, Kellenbeck gagged again and vomited through his hands—and propelled him into Greene and all three of us sandwichlike out onto the deck. The gun fired, cracking, but Greene's arm had been thrown out to the side; the bullet hummed off into the night. He went down with Kellenbeck sprawled half on top of him, still yelling, kicking viciously to free himself. I stayed on my feet—but momentum and the deck-roll flung me off-balance against the starboard gunwale.

Greene got his arm free, swung the gun around.

I threw myself overboard.

NINETEEN

The gun cracked again just as I cleared the gunwale. I felt a hard slapping along the edge of my right shoe; the leg jerked in reflex and the knee bent up against my chest, and that made my body, already twisted into an awkward position, curl around instead of flattening out as I fell. I hit the water on my neck and right shoulder with enough impact to flip me over, slice me backward through the surface.

It was like dropping naked into a snowdrift. The subfreezing temperature constricted my lungs, deflated them in a convulsive exhalation. Brackish water streamed into my mouth before I could snap it closed again. I fought to get my legs down and under me, body turned into a horizontal plane. But by the time I managed that the pressure in my chest was acute and painful; I had to have air—and I had to orient myself—before I could start to swim.

154

I stopped thrashing arms and legs, let the water's buoyancy bob me up like a cork. When my head broke surface I opened my mouth wide and filled my lungs in gasping breaths. Salt stung my eyes, laid a film across them; at first I could not see anything except smeary blackness. Then the movement of the water shuttled me half-around, and on my left I could make out a blurred shimmer of red and green: the *Kingfisher's* running lights. I blinked half a dozen times until the lights steadied into focus. The boat was a dark shape that seemed to be floating spectrally in fog, maybe twenty yards away and still angled away from the marina. No movement on the deck astern—which had to mean that Greene was up and inside the wheelhouse, about to swing the troller around.

I struggled, kicking again, to face the opposite direction. More shapes loomed up through the mist: boats rocking in the marina slips. How far away? Seventy-five yards? A hundred?

Trapped air had billowed my overcoat around me; I ripped at the buttons and wrenched out of it. And at the same time scraped off my waterlogged shoes. Behind me I could hear the guttural throb of the diesel climb in volume. I twisted my head to look back there.

The boat was thirty yards away now and just starting into a tight left-hand turn.

I scissored up and into a rapid crawl. The direction of the wind and what current there was were in my favor; I did not have to fight through the swells. But the water was freezing cold: Before long my arms and legs began to numb, to feel heavy, and I was forced to shorten and slow my stroke. Each breath burned as if I were inhaling slivers of dry ice.

Don't think about the cold. Swim!

Stroke.

Stroke.

Head up: The marina was maybe thirty or forty yards distant now. I could see the dull fuzzy glow of the nightlights, the end of the center float, the entrances to the two channels on either side.

Stroke.

Stroke.

Stroke—

Off to my left a beam of light sprayed out over the water; the throb of the diesel seemed to build to a roaring. I rolled onto my side, dragged my head around again.

The troller was fifteen yards behind me, coming at about quarter-throttle but at an angle to the west. The hand-operated spotlight probed around in an arc, glistening off streamers of fog. Greene had not seen me yet—but it would only be a matter of seconds until he did.

I sucked in as much air as I could hold and took myself under, just as the beam swung closer and the bow veered toward me.

When I had kicked straight down for maybe ten feet I swam in a blind forward breaststroke. In my mind I counted off ten seconds, fifteen. The amount of salt in the water kept trying to buoy me up; my arms felt as if there were lead sinkers tied to them and a cramp was starting to form in the calf of my left leg.

Twenty seconds.

And the troller passed above me—not directly overhead but close enough so that I could hear the water-muffled whine of the diesel, feel the turbulence created by the screws.

I made myself count off another five seconds. Then I clawed upward, broke surface just as the pressure mounted to an intolerable level in my chest; my lungs heaved, the intake of air sent out shoots of pain. The *Kingfisher's* wake pitched me around like a piece of flotsam, the salt film and rivulets of water obscured my vision. I shook my head, breathing in pants and gulps. Had to shake it twice more before I could see where the boat was: between me and the marina, twenty yards away and running diagonally to my left.

I kicked out and swam half a dozen uneven strokes. Struggled clear of the wake with my head up and my eyes fixed on the troller. It turned perpendicular to the marina and then began to veer around hard right; the spotlight sliced a down-slanted arc through the blackness, swinging toward me. I dragged in air and tensed for another dive.

But then the bow straightened, and I saw that the boat was

going to bypass me this time by a good fifteen yards. The light jerked back the other way. Greene had no idea where I was; he was hunting blind in the fog. I stopped swimming and treaded water, so that only my head bobbed above the surface. I was afraid of giving my position away with splashes and churned-up foam.

The *Kingfisher* drew abreast—and growled past without changing trajectory.

I lowered my head, flailed out again. The cramp in my calf was worse now: hot wire of pain jabbing all the way up to the hip.

Stroke.

Stroke.

Leg stiffening up.

Stroke.

Agony.

Stroke.

How much farther? Head up. More of the center float visible, boat moored in the right-hand slip rearing up black but distinct, left-hand slip empty. Twenty yards, maybe less.

Stroke.

Leg on fire.

Stroke.

The diesel sound—I could no longer hear it except as a low rumble. Greene, the boat, where were they now?

Drifting in the swells forty or fifty yards distant.

Throttle shut off, just drifting.

Movement on deck near the starboard gunwale; a mass of heavy shadows, distorted by the fog. Then they seemed to separate, amoebalike. I thought I saw a blackish lump drop down over the side, thought I heard a splash.

Kellenbeck? Dead, dumped overboard?

Swim!

Flex the leg, suck in air, crawl forward. Pain. Numbness. Heart hammering in a wild cadence. Not enough air; gasps and whimpers coming out of my throat.

Stroke.

Stroke.

Less than ten yards.

Stroke.

Engine sound climbing again.

Leg locked up, useless, can't swim anymore—

—dog-paddle then, dog-paddle—

—almost there, *get* there—

—and the edge of the float came up in front of me and I hauled one leaden arm out of the water and fumbled at the slick wood, felt the sharp rib of a barnacle cut into my palm. Got a grip on the upper rim of the float and hung on, pulling myself in against it.

Behind me the throb of the diesel grew louder.

I managed to get both forearms onto the float, tried to heave myself up out of the water. But I had no strength left; my whole body trembled with exhaustion and the pain in my leg was hellish. Clinging there, I twisted to look back over my shoulder.

The spotlight and the *Kingfisher's* bow were pointed straight toward the marina channel a few yards to my left.

Get away from here, I thought, get into the other channel.

Fingers clawing at the boards, I pulled myself toward the right-hand corner of the float. The troller was nearing the channel; Greene throttled down and I saw the black hull buck in the swells, the bow drift left until he corrected. The light flicked toward me—

I heaved around to the channel side just before it swept over the float. Pulled my hands down and shoved the palms against the barnacled underside to hold my head low in the water, beneath the float's upper edge. Above and beyond me, the light illuminated the rigging and wheelhouse of the boat moored in the near slip. And then cut away as the *Kingfisher* passed into the channel.

Some of the desperation faded; my mind was sluggish, but I had control of it. Control of my breathing too. I pushed up, dragged forward to the inner corner. Heard the troller's engines whine into reverse. Heading into his slip, I thought. But then what? Did Greene think I was still somewhere out in the bay?

That I had drowned? That I had made it in here? He might just leave the boat and make for Kellenbeck's Cadillac—but it was more likely he would take that flashlight of his and prowl the floats, searching for me.

Stay where I was, hide under the float if he came this way, wait him out? No good. The numbness was spreading and I was beginning to feel almost warm; I knew what that meant well enough. The frigid water had robbed me of body heat: Another few minutes and I would no longer be able to feel or do anything, I would lose consciousness, I would freeze and then drown. I *had* to get out of the water, even if it meant exposing myself. And I had to do it in the next minute or so, before Greene finished docking the *Kingfisher*.

I anchored both forearms on the float again, squirmed upward. But my shoulder and back muscles, and the lower half of my body, were so weak it was like trying to boost up a two-hundred-pound slab of meat; I managed to get my breastbone over the edge and that was all. I hung there, kicking with my good leg, straining frantically to keep from sliding backward.

The engine sound decreased to an idling rumble: Greene had maneuvered into his slip.

I threw my right arm out, clutched at the float's inner edge to hold myself in position—and my chilled fingers brushed over a rusted iron ring imbedded there, part of a rope tied through it. Cleat. And the bow line on the boat above me. I caught hold of the rope and tugged on it. The boat made a creaking noise, rocked forward; the line slackened enough for me to get it looped once around my wrist. Then I put my left hand down flat on the boards, heaved up, pulled back on the rope at the same time. Flopped my body from side to side. Heaved, pulled, flopped until my chest, stomach, abdomen cleared the edge—

—and I was out of the water and dragging myself forward, knees scraping over the rough wood.

Across the opposite channel the *Kingfisher's* spotlight and running lights winked out. The diesel shut down. Silence settled around me, broken only by the fog bells and the wheezing plaint of my breathing.

Thin gusts of wind stung my face, cut through the numbness and took away the false feeling of warmth; I began to shake with chills as I lifted back into a kneeling position. When I got my right foot planted and a two-handed grip on the bow line I hoisted and levered myself upright. Almost fell when I tried to put weight on the cramped leg; it buckled and pitched me sideways against the boat. I let go of the rope, grabbed onto the gunwale to steady myself.

The wheelhouse blocked off my view of Greene's slip. Blocked off his view, too. Nothing stirred in any other direction except tracers and puffs of fog. I swung myself on board, good leg first, and hobbled to the port wheelhouse bulkhead. Eased along it and around to the aft side.

Unlike Greene's, this wheelhouse had a door; it was shut, but when I depressed the latch it popped open. Into the heavy blackness inside. Shut the door again. Down on all fours so I would not bang into anything and make a carrying noise. Then I crawled over to the helm and lifted up to peer through the mist-streaked windshield.

The pale nightlights let me see part of the float where Greene's slip was. And he was there, moving away from the ramp toward the bay end. Going to look for me, all right. Near the end he stopped and raised his arm: A shaft of light stabbed out from that big flash of his, swept back and forth in a restless arc over the water. Pretty soon he turned onto the right-angled outer arm, shone the beam across the channel toward where I was. I ducked down, stayed down until the hazy glow disappeared from the glass.

When I raised up again he was hurrying back toward the ramp. I might have lost sight of him in the fog except that he still had the flash switched on; I could see it flicking out between the moored boats—and I could follow it all the way past the ramp and around onto the connecting walkway.

Coming out here, too.

I crawled back along the bulkhead, feeling with my hands. Storage locker aft, near the door—but it was padlocked. I groped above it. Touched cold metal that my fingers told me was a wood-handled steel hook, attached to the bulkhead with clips. Gaff, for hooking and holding heavy fish. Weapon. I took it down, crept back under the wheel. Knelt there gripping it across my chest.

The sodden clothing clung like a wrapping of ice; tremors racked me and I had to lock my teeth together to keep them from chattering. The cramp had loosened a little, but the leg still ached. All of me ached: muscles, joints, bones. My face was stiff with saltcake; the rest of my skin had a puckered feel, cold and hot at the same time, as if with fever.

Pneumonia, I thought.

Flickers of light shone beyond the windshield, went on past. Muffled slap of Greene's shoes on the float outside. Could he tell I had come out of the water there, climbed on board this boat? No. Float was already wet, sloshed over, and the deck was wet too from the dripping mist. He might decide to check out each of the moored boats, but that wasn't likely; take too much time, and he could not be sure of what had happened to me. For all he knew I had made it to shore and was already on my way to summon the cops. He just could not afford to hang around much longer.

Another ten seconds passed.

Come on, you son of a bitch. Move out, start running.

Ten more seconds.

Light in the glass again, centered there for an instant. Then it moved off. Footfalls, fading.

Darkness except for the nightlights.

Silence.

I let out a breath through my nostrils. But stayed where I was for a time, listening. Still no sounds from outside. Raised up again, leaned close to the windshield. Emptiness across the way, no movement of any kind. Faint movement of light far down to the right, though, reflected off the fog—Greene over on the float?

Half a minute. Forty seconds.

And the beam reappeared, hazed and steady, on the walkway at the shore end. Moved along there and around onto the westside float, dancing out again between the boats. Stopped at the *Kingfisher*, traced a path up across the deck, splashed over the wheelhouse. Probed inside. Vanished.

More waiting, face pressed close to the glass. One minute. Two. Three. The light poked back out, retraced across the deck and down onto the float. Shut off again in front of the ramp. Four beats. Black silhouette: Greene climbing up the metal ladder, something large and squarish in his right hand. Suitcase?

Then he was gone, swallowed by the mist and the darkness.

I used the gaff as a fulcrum to push myself onto my feet. Left leg took my weight now, but I would have to favor the right just in case. I leaned against the binnacle, staring out. More waiting, to make sure he didn't decide to come back.

Emptiness.

Okay, enough. Enough. Back along the bulkhead to the door, out on deck. Over the gunwale, still hanging onto the gaff, and down the float to the connecting walkway.

Stillness.

Around to the ramp. Up the ladder in cautious movements, to peer down the ramp at the highway.

Deserted highway: Kellenbeck's Cadillac was gone.

Onto the ramp, along the ramp. Stumbling a little now; legs wobbly, threatening to give out. The wind welding clothing to skin, making me shake like a man with palsy.

Drop the gaff, cross the road. Packed-dirt driveway there, leading up to where houselights glowed behind the screen of fog. Up the driveway. Stumbling again, falling, getting up. House taking shape—gray hexagonal thing with a wrap around porch and switchback stairs leading up. Climb the stairs, lean panting beside the door. Knock on the door. Somebody coming, somebody opening up—

And it was over.

God—it was over.

TWENTY

The next few hours were a time I lived through with a kind of schizoid detachment: part of me seemed to retreat, to become a disinterested observer, while the other part continued to operate more or less normally. Temporary reactional dysfunction, the psychologists call it, induced by a period of intense physical and emotional stress. And the hell with them and their fancy labels.

The people who lived in the house were the Muhlheims, a couple of artists in their forties. They were helpful and solicitous types and the first thing they tried to do was to get me out of my wet clothes; but all I could think about was using the phone. Muhlheim wrapped a blanket around me while I called the county police in Santa Rosa. I used Eberhardt's and Donleavy's names to get through to a lieutenant named Fitzpatrick and laid out the story for him in clipped sentences, some of which I had to repeat because of the way my teeth kept clacking together; the only thing I omitted was mention of the private eye as a horse's ass: my breaking into the Kellenbeck Fish Company. Fitzpatrick asked a couple of terse questions, and my answers and the urgency in my voice seemed to convince him I was telling a straight story. He instructed me to stay where I was, said he would take care of contacting other police agencies.

When I hung up I let Muhlheim show me to the bathroom. He and his wife had listened to my end of the conversation with plenty of interest, but to his credit he did not try to question me. He gave me some dry clothes—we were about the same size—and left me alone to strip and take a five-minute, steaming-hot shower. Which only just dulled the edge of my chill, but which at least stopped the shaking.

Mrs. Muhlheim had a pot of hot tea and another blanket waiting when I came out. Plus some salve for the barnacle cuts on my hands. Ten more minutes passed, most of it in silence; the tea warmed me a little more. Then there was a sharp rapping on the front door. And things began to happen.

Two highway patrolmen. Questions. A guy from the Coast Guard station at Doran Park. A pair of county Sheriff's deputies. More questions. Another highway patrolman. A telephone call to Santa Rosa made by one of the deputies. And after that they took me out of there, bundled in an old overcoat offered up by Muhlheim, and down to the Highway Patrol substation south of Bodega.

Fitzpatrick, a youngish guy with an authoritarian manner, arrived from Santa Rosa. More questions. Report from the Coast Guard: They had fished Kellenbeck's body out of the bay near the marina, shot once through the heart. A doctor showed up, summoned by somebody along the line, and spent a little time examining me. No fever, he said, no other signs of incipient pneumonia. He gave me some pills to swallow, told me to see my physician if I developed any serious symptoms, and went away.

Eberhardt called from his home—Fitzpatrick had notified the Hall of Justice and they in turn had contacted Eb—and I was allowed to talk to him. In concerned tones he asked how I was. I said I was fine, wonderful, that son of a bitch Greene had come within minutes of killing me dead. Then I told the story all over again, for the fifth or sixth time. I'll get back to you in the morning, he said. Yeah, I said.

Greene was still at large. But there was an All-Points Bulletin out on him, Fitzpatrick told me—it was only a matter of time. The head of the Alcohol and Firearms Unit office in San Francisco called. I got to talk to him, too, and answer some more questions, and listen to him tell me he would send agents up in the morning to interrogate me "when you're feeling better."

I was so tired by this time, from all the talk and the pills and the physical and mental strain, that I had trouble holding my head up. I asked Fitzpatrick if I could please, for Christ's sake, be taken somewhere so I could get some sleep. Yes, he supposed I had been through enough for one night. Damned right, I thought. Put you up at The Tides Motel, somebody said, that okay? Just dandy.

Out of there finally and into a car, Fitzpatrick driving. Where was my car? he asked. Up by the Kellenbeck Fish Company. Keys? Lost in the bay, they were in my overcoat pocket, but there's another set in a little magnetic box behind the rear bumper. He'd have somebody pick it up and bring it to the motel.

Motel. Check-in. Room. They went away, saying they would talk to me again in the morning. Bed. Sleep. Dreams of ice and water, guns and darkness, dead faces floating at the bottom of the sea.

Long, bad night . . .

A knocking on the door woke me. I sat up a little groggily and it took me a few seconds to orient myself, remember where I was. Gray light in the room, filtering in through half-closed drapes over the window. I squinted at my watch. It was a good old waterproof Timex and still ticking away, undamaged by the salt water last night; the hands read eight-twenty-five.

I swung my feet out, sat on the edge of the bed. The knocking came again. I called, "Just a minute," and then stood up in a tentative way, testing my legs. Stiff, with a faint weakness in the joints. Same feeling in my arms. My head was stuffy and there was congestion in my lungs, the kind I used to have before I gave up cigarettes. Otherwise I seemed to be in reasonably good shape for what I had been through.

I put on Muhlheim's clothes and went over and opened the door. Fitzpatrick. He asked me how I was, but not as if it mattered a great deal to him, and handed me my car keys.

"Greene?" I said.

He shook his head. "Not yet. But we'll get him, don't worry."

"I'm not worried. Just eager."

"Sure. Federal agents are here; they said they'd be over to see you later this morning. So don't go anywhere for awhile."

"How about after I see them? Can I leave for home then?"

"You can as far as I'm concerned," Fitzpatrick said. "But stop by the substation before you go; there's a statement waiting for you to sign."

After he left I went into the bathroom and looked at myself in the mirror. Beard stubble, puffy eyes, mottled skin, hair sticking up every which way like a fright wig: face to scare little children with. I turned out of there, put on Muhlheim's overcoat, left the room, and hunted up my car. Reversed the procedure, carrying my overnight case, and then went to work on the beard stubble with a razor.

While I shaved I did some heavy thinking for the first time since early last night. Not about Greene and what had happened in the bay; that brush with death, and my own foolishness that had led to it, was something I did not want to relive. What I did think about was the bootlegging and the murders of Jerry Carding and his father. And about all the questions that were still unanswered, the one major question that was still unanswered.

Who had murdered Christine Webster?

The mental work got me nowhere. And yet, if I kept going over things enough times, maybe there was something I knew and could remember—like the little things I had known and remembered about Kellenbeck and the Cardings. Maybe . . .

The telephone rang just as I finished toweling off. I went into the other room, picked up the receiver. And listened to Eberhardt's voice say, "It's me. How you feeling this morning?"

"Fair. Better than I ought to."

"No after effects?"

"None I want to talk about."

"Yeah," he said. "Guy in the Highway Patrol office up there told me where you were. According to him, no word on Greene yet."

"I know. Fitzpatrick came by a few minutes ago."

"You wouldn't be planning to stick around up there until he's caught?"

"Hell no. I'll be home as soon as they're done with me."

"When'll that be?"

"Sometime this afternoon, I guess. I've got to go sign a statement. And see a couple of Federal agents before that."

"Me too," he said. "I just got off the phone with one of the Alcohol and Firearms boys."

"Have you talked to Donleavy?"

"Little while ago."

"Is he dropping the charges against Martin Talbot?"

"That's what he says. But the Carding murder is still officially open until Greene turns up. Or some kind of incriminating evidence does." He paused. "The Christine Webster case is still open too, damn it."

"Greene didn't kill her, Eb," I said.

"So you managed to tell me last night. You're probably right—but I'd like it better if you weren't."

"I would too. But there's just no motive for him to've shot the girl. Jerry Carding only had two copies of his article the night he was killed; there wasn't a third he could have mailed to Christine."

"Greene might have been afraid he'd told her something," Eberhardt said, "and went after her for that reason."

"It doesn't add up. Why would Greene be more worried about

167

Christine than, say, Steve Farmer or Sharon Darden—people right here at Bodega Bay? And if he had wanted to kill her, why wait until Tuesday night to do it? And why shoot her with a .32 instead of the .38 he used on Carding or the Browning automatic he tried to use on me?"

Eberhardt sighed. "I can't argue with any of that," he said. "All right, Greene didn't kill Christine. But then who did? And why? Where's the connection?"

"Maybe there isn't one. Not a direct one, anyway."

"Coincidence?"

"That's what I'm thinking."

"I don't like coincidences worth a damn."

"Neither do I, usually. But they do happen, Eb. They even happen in bunches sometimes."

"Bunches?"

"I'm starting to wonder," I said, "if maybe there aren't a lot of coincidences in these two cases."

"Meaning what? You got another theory?"

"No. Just a feeling so far. Did you dig up anything on Bobbie Reid, by the way?"

"Not much. She was the private type: no close friends, kept pretty much to herself. Her parents live in Red Bluff and they're the ones who claimed the body; neither of them had much contact with Bobbie in the past year, said they didn't know why she committed suicide. Didn't seem too broken up about it, either. Nice folks."

"What about the people where she worked?"

"Same thing. She was a legal secretary in a law office downtown; none of her coworkers knew her very well. Her boss, Arthur Brown, says he'd been thinking about firing her just before her death—late for work on a regular basis, withdrawn, moody, fouled up an important brief. . . . " Pause. "Hold on a second, will you?" He covered the mouthpiece but I could hear muffled voices in the background. A few seconds later he came back on. "I've got to go; the Alcohol and Firearms people are here. Call me when you get back to the city."

"I may call you sooner than that," I said.

"What?"

"Maybe inside an hour."

"What the hell are you talking about?"

"I'm not sure yet. I'll get back to you when I am."

I rang off and went over and stood looking out through the bayside window. More fog today, swirling heavily over the ruffled surface of the bay. Like the thoughts swirling over the surface of my mind. Facts, memory scraps, additions and subtractions—all swirling and then beginning to coalesce into the missing part of the blueprint.

For the first time, then, I could see the complete design of the labyrinth. And it only had three connecting sides. The open end, the missing side, was nothing but coincidence—multiple coincidence.

Our stubborn refusal to accept that, particularly on this kind of *Grand Guignol* basis, was what had been hanging us up all along. Part of everything had begun with accidental occurrence and some of the complications had been built on it: a car driven by Martin Talbot crashing into one driven by Victor Carding; Christine Webster having my business card and Laura Nichols deciding she needed a private detective; Talbot and me arriving at the Carding house just after Carding's murder; all the suicides real and attempted and bogus; interrelationships among the people involved; even things like Greene showing up at Kellenbeck's house just in time to spot me last night. Three parts connective tissue to one part coincidence.

I thought I knew now who had killed Christine and I had a hunch as to why. But I needed the answer to one more question before I could be sure. Just one more question.

I put on Muhlheim's coat again, went out and down across the parking lot. The cold wind made my eyes water and started my nose running; my chest still felt badly congested. If I was smart I would make an appointment tomorrow with Doctor White. The shape my lungs were in, pneumonia was a threat I could not afford to overlook.

Inside The Tides Wharf I walked around into the warehouse area behind the fish market. Deserted. I came back out to the counter where a balding guy in a white apron was fileting salmon and asked him if Steve Farmer had reported for work today. The guy said yes, he was in the restaurant on his break.

So I crossed over there and stepped inside. Farmer was sitting at one of the tables near the windows; he was alone and seemed to be brooding into a cup of coffee. When I went to him and said, "Hello, Steve," he looked up at me with pained and listless eyes.

"Oh," he said, "it's you."

I sat down. "I guess you know about Jerry."

"I heard this morning. It's all people are talking about."

"I'm sorry it had to turn out this way."

"Sure." He stared into the cup. "Jerry too," he said. "All of them—just like I was afraid it would be."

Yeah, I thought, all of them. But I said, "I need the answer to a question, Steve. You're the only person who can give it to me."

"What question?"

"Why did Bobbie Reid commit suicide?"

His face started to close up again, the way it had before, but this time it did not quite make it—as if Jerry Carding's death had taken the edge off his feelings about everything else. He rested an elbow on the table, cocked the hand against his forehead like a visor. "Why do you have to keep bugging me about Bobbie? It's all finished now, for God's sake. Her suicide doesn't have anything to do with the murders."

"Yes it does. It's got everything to do with Christine Webster's murder."

He gave me an anguished look from under the visored hand. "But I thought Andy Greene and Gus Kellenbeck—?"

"No. They killed Jerry and his father, yes. But not Christine." I paused and then asked him again, in a gentler tone: "Why did Bobbie commit suicide?"

"I don't know, not for sure. She had hangups. . . ."

"What hangups? Steve, why did you break up with her?"

"I didn't. She broke up with me; she . . . found somebody else. . . ."

170

"Who?"

"I don't know. Somebody *else*, that's all."

"Another man?"

His shoulders sagged; he dropped both forearms to the table edge and slumped over them with his head bent. "No," he said, "not another man. She was making it with a woman. I loved her and she turned gay on me, she turned into a lesbian. . . ."

Bingo.

TWENTY-ONE

I called Eberhardt back ten minutes later and laid it all out
for him: who I believed had shot Christine Webster and why.
He said it sounded reasonable but he would need proof, not
speculation and hearsay, before he could make an arrest; but he
agreed with me that he would not have too much trouble finding
it. With luck he could have the whole ugly business wrapped
up by the end of the day.

The Justice Department investigators showed up not long
afterward, and I spent two hours making another statement and
answering an endless string of questions. When they were finally
done with me I had a headache and an achey feeling in my
joints; but I also had their permission to go back to San Francisco.
Twelve minutes after they left I was on my way to the Highway
Patrol substation. And twenty minutes after that I was on my

way home—sniffling and hacking up phlegm with the heater on full blast.

It was a few minutes past three when I crossed the Golden Gate Bridge. The fog there was as thick as it had been up the coast; you could not see the bridge towers or much of Alcatraz or Angel Island, and the hills and buildings of the city had a gray distorted look. But that was all right. I liked the fog more than ever now, because without it I would not have survived last night's ordeal with Greene.

I drove down Lombard, straight up Laguna. Predictably, the closest parking space to my building turned out to be two blocks away. My joints ached even more now and I had developed a scratchy throat; the two-block walk in the cold did me no good at all.

I gathered up my mail and let myself in. When I got up to my door I felt a twinge of apprehension, remembering what I had found at my office on Friday. But both locks were secure and nothing had been disturbed inside: the pulps were still on their shelves, the bachelor's mess on the furniture and floor was just as I had left it.

Brew up some tea, I thought, take another cold pill, and get into bed. So I threw Muhlheim's coat on the couch—I would have to remember to get the coat and the rest of his clothing cleaned and shipped back to him pretty soon—and headed toward the kitchen.

On the way I shuffled through the mail. And one of the envelopes made me stop in the doorway. It was plain-white and business-sized, with no return address. And the "r" in my name was chipped, the "a" in the street address tilted.

Christ. I tore it open, pulled out a single sheet of white paper, and unfolded it. My name was typed there, too, and below it three lines:

> You'd better leave me alone. If you
> don't, I'll do something to YOU next time,
> not just your office. I mean that. Leave
> me ALONE.

I held up the envelope and looked at the postmark. Mailed Saturday night. Sure, that figured. She must have written it right after my call—

Somebody knocked on the door.

Frowning, I turned to look over there. Dennis Litchak, probably, because the downstairs door buzzer had not sounded; he must have seen or heard me enter and come up to talk. Well, I was in no mood or condition for company right now. I went to the door, thinking that I would get rid of old Dennis in five seconds flat, and opened up.

Karen Nichols stood in the hallway outside.

"I've been waiting for you all day," she said. "Waiting and waiting for you. I thought you'd never come home."

In her right hand was a .32 caliber revolver.

The muscles in my stomach and groin contracted; I could feel heat come into my cheeks and a shaking start up inside. This was the second time in eighteen hours that a gun had been pointed at me, that I had tasted sudden fear and come up against sudden death. It had been bad enough with Greene, but this was worse because I was sick and exhausted and because it meant coping all over again, trying to beat the odds twice in a row.

I still had hold of the door and I considered throwing it shut, diving out of the way. But I would have had to step back to do that, to get the door in front of my body and my reflexes were shaky and not to be trusted. She had already moved forward to the threshold, too, and her finger was tight against the trigger. Too risky. Stay calm, I told myself, find another way. Don't do anything to make her shoot.

"Back up and let me in," she said. "Somebody might come."

I let go of the door, retreated in slow careful steps. She came inside and pushed the door almost shut behind her with her free hand. Her face was so pale that I could see the fine tracery of veins beneath the skin, but there was nothing in her expression or in the wide amber eyes to indicate how unbalanced she was. She looked normal, in full control of herself, and that scared me even more than if she'd been wild-eyed and gibbering. She could errupt into violence at any second, on the slightest provocation—the way she must have when she destroyed my office.

She said, "You got my letter," and I realized I still had it and the envelope and the rest of the mail in my left hand.

"Yes. I got it."

"I shouldn't have sent it. I shouldn't have sent any of the letters to that Webster bitch either. They didn't do any good. Nothing does any good. Except this." She raised the gun slightly and looked at it as if it were a new-found friend, an ally. "This is the only way."

"You don't want to shoot me, Karen," I said.

"Yes I do. I have to. You won't leave me alone. I thought if I went to your office last week and talked to you . . . but you weren't there, and I thought if I went in and did things to it, it would hurt you enough to make you go away. But you didn't, you just kept on and on. When you asked me about Bobbie on Saturday night I knew what I had to do. I knew this was the only way. I waited for you all afternoon and all evening. And all day today. Why didn't you come home?"

Without moving my head much I looked left, right—but I was standing in the middle of the carpet and there was nothing in a five-foot radius that I could use to disarm her. The nearest piece of furniture was the couch, three paces to my right. And nothing on it except the overcoat, a pulp magazine, a couple of throw pillows.

"Karen, listen to me—"

"No. I don't want to listen. I just want to do what I have to before it's too late."

Throw pillows. *Throw* pillow?

"It's already too late," I said. "The police know the truth."

Her forehead puckered; she bit her lip. "I don't believe you."

Long odds. Even if I could get over to the couch, pick up one of the pillows, it would take a perfect toss to hit the gun before she fired, throw her off-balance long enough for me to rush her.

But what other choice did I have? It seemed to be either that or try to jump her cold.

I said, "It's true, Karen. The police have been out to your house today, they've matched the typing on the letters with the typewriter in your living room; they know you wrote them to Christine."

"I don't believe you," she said again.

"Why would I lie to you?"

"Because you want to hurt me. Along with my mother and that Webster bitch. Won't go away, won't stop hurting me . . ."

Her jaw trembled a little and her eyes were brighter; you could see the violence rippling like a dark current just beneath the surface of her face. The knotted feeling in my groin intensified. Keep her talking, for God's sake, I thought. But don't say anything to provoke her.

"I never wanted to hurt you, Karen. I only wanted to help your uncle."

"No. You were working for Webster all along."

"But I wasn't," I said, and took a careful sidestep toward the couch. The gun did not move in her hand. "Christine never contacted me. I never met her or talked to her."

"You're lying again. She had your business card. And she *told* me she'd hired you, just before I did it to her."

That did not surprise me. The reason why Christine had lied was obvious: she had been trying desperately to save her life. And the lie explained how Karen had known I was a detective when I arrived at her house on Wednesday morning. I had only given her my name at the door, not my occupation, and by their own testimony Laura Nichols had not told her daughter of her plans to hire an investigator. Yet the first thing Karen had said to me was, "You're that private detective."

"Working for Webster," she said now, "and then right away going to work for my mother. Don't you think I know the real reason *she* hired you?"

"I don't know what you mean. Your mother hired me to watch over your uncle."

"That was just a lie for my benefit. She hired you to investigate *me*."

"Why would she do that?"

"She hates me, that's why. She suspected I was gay. She suspected I was in love with Bobbie and wanted to hurt the bitch who killed her. She hired you so you could both work against me."

Paranoid psychosis, I thought. Everybody out to harm her, including her mother. Especially her mother. She was the one with all the hatred, not Laura Nichols; and those feelings had to be at the root of her persecution complex and her need to strike back.

I took another step toward the couch. My nose was running again, dripping down over my upper lip; I sniffled and just let it drip. No use pressing my luck by reaching into the back pocket where my handkerchief was.

"Your mother didn't tell me about you and Bobbie," I said. "She doesn't know you're gay."

"She must have told you. You weren't surprised when I said it just now. You already knew."

"Yes. But I found out another way—"

"*She* told you. Stop lying to me."

Easy, I thought, drop it right there. Because the truth was provocative: it was Karen herself who had told me. On the phone Thursday night she'd said she and some friends had spent the day at Civic Center and I remembered noticing in Friday's paper that at Civic Center on Thursday there had been a big Gay Rights rally. And when I had talked to her Saturday night from Bodega Bay and asked if she knew Bobbie Reid, she'd said, "No. Who's she?" Yet Bobbie, or Bobby, is a far more common male name than a female name; the assumption almost everybody makes the first time they hear it is that it's short for Robert, not Roberta or Barbara. Which indicated Karen *had* known Bobbie Reid. Add those facts together, along with Eberhardt's news that Bobbie had worked for Arthur Brown, the Nichols' family attorney, and Steve Farmer's admission that Bobbie was gay, and the truth became clear enough.

"Well?" she said. "My mother told you, didn't she?"

"Yes."

"And you think being gay is terrible, don't you. Just like she does."

"No, I don't think it's terrible."

"Are you lying to me again?"

"No. I think every person has the right to be what he wants to be. As long as he doesn't harm anyone else."

"Webster harmed Bobbie. *Killed* her, the bitch."

"How did she do that?"

"With words. Words. Bobbie never told anyone about us; she was confused about being gay. But Webster got it out of her. She told Bobbie it was evil and she was sick and needed help. Kept telling her again and again. Bobbie couldn't take it. She was a sensitive person and she just . . . she couldn't take it. She took those pills, and she called me afterward to say she was sorry, she had to do it, she couldn't cope anymore after what Webster had been telling her. I told her how much I loved her, I begged her not to do it, but she said it was too late. I called the emergency hospital, I drove over there myself, and it was. It was too late. . . ."

Poor Bobbie Reid: emotionally screwed up, unable to come to terms with her life and her sexuality—a probable suicide in any case. Poor Christine Webster: well-meaning, foolish, always trying to meddle in other people's lives. Victims, just like Jerry Carding. Poor Karen, too: unbalanced, deluded, filled with paranoid hatred for her domineering mother. She was another victim, and I pitied her a little in that moment. But I pitied Jerry and Christine and Bobbie a great deal more.

Karen seemed to be caught up for the moment in memory and grief; the gun was steady but no longer pointing straight at me. I took another step that brought me up next to the couch. But the movement alerted her, made her blink and swing the weapon back dead-center on my chest.

"Don't move," she said. "Why are you moving?"

I stood motionless, watching the gun. "I want to sit down. Is that all right?"

Hesitation. Then, "I don't care. I'm going to do what I have to pretty soon. Like I did with Webster. I wish I could do it to my mother too. But I can't. I want to but I . . . can't. Not yet."

I eased myself down on the arm of the couch, let my right arm dangle down at my side. The closest of the throw pillows was eight or nine inches away: I would have to lean in that direction in order to reach it.

"How did you do it to Webster?" I said. "How did you get her to meet you at Lake Merced?"

"Why do you want to know that?"

"I just do. Will you tell me?"

"I called her on the phone, that's how. Not like the other calls, where I disguised my voice. I said I knew who was threatening her, but I didn't want to say anything on the phone and I was afraid to come to her apartment because the person might be watching her. I asked her to meet me and she said she would. She thought it was a *man* who wanted to hurt her, you see; she wasn't afraid of me. But I made her afraid. I made her very afraid before I did it to her."

A feeling of nausea formed inside me: her words, tension, suppressed fear. I tipped my body to the right, moved my arm out away from it—one inch, two, three.

"I thought it was all done with then," she said. "Webster did it to Bobbie, I did it to Webster. But then you came. And there were all those lies about Uncle Martin. And Victor Carding was murdered. And I found out Jerry Carding was his son and Webster's boyfriend too. I never knew that before. I never even heard of Jerry Carding. It confused me, I couldn't understand what was happening."

Coincidence, that was what had been happening. Martin Talbot and Victor Carding have an accident; Carding's son is Christine Webster's fiance; Talbot's niece is having an affair with Bobbie Reid; Bobbie Reid is a friend of Christine's and used to date a friend of Jerry Carding's; Christine finds out Bobbie is gay and admonishes her for it; Bobbie commits suicide; Karen blames Christine and murders her. And Bobbie works in Arthur Brown's law office; Christine works part-time in the same building; Brown is Laura Nichols' attorney; I've done some work for Brown and always hand out cards to my clients; Christine gets one of the cards from Brown; Laura Nichols wants to hire a private detective and Brown recommends me. A crazy-quilt of coincidence.

But there was no point in saying any of that to Karen; she would not have believed it. I stayed silent and kept leaning toward the throw pillow. Four inches. Five.

"Then I did understand," she said. "It was somebody *else* working against me. Not just you and my mother, but Jerry Carding too. He knew I was the one who hurt Webster and he did it to his own father so Uncle Martin would be blamed. That was his way of hurting me back."

Six. Seven—

Sound out in the hallway.

I froze, listening, staring at Karen. She seemed not to have heard it: a footstep, muffled by the carpeting out there. One of the Madisons, the couple who lived in the other flat on this floor?

"If I knew where Jerry Carding was, I'd do it to him too. I'd make him leave me alone."

Behind her a crack opened between the door and jamb; she had not closed the door all the way so there was no click of the latch opening, no sound at all. I straightened away from the pillow, leaned forward instead. Every muscle and nerve in my body felt coiled.

"I'll make everybody leave me alone. I don't believe you about the police; they don't know yet. Only you and Mother and Jerry Carding know."

The crack widened a little more. A head poked around the edge of the door.

Dennis Litchak.

"You first and then Jerry Carding when I can find him. Then my mother someday. Then I'll be safe—"

The hinges squeaked. She heard the sound this time and her face registered surprise; reflex made her jerk her head around to look behind her, made the gun swing away from me.

I levered up off the couch and threw myself at her.

The damned gun went off, the lamp on the sideboard near the kitchen shattered, the door banged shut, I hit her with my shoulder and sent her reeling back against the wall. She caromed off, crying out in a hurt way, and the gun flew clear of her hand and skittered under the writing desk; she went down and rolled over and lay in a quivering little heap.

I veered away from her, went to one knee beside the desk, and scooped up the gun. When I straightened with it, the tension went out of me all at once, like a balloon deflating, and I had to lean against the desk top to keep from falling down.

Karen stopped quivering and lifted onto her knees. Looked at me with eyes that had gone dull with pain and confusion. "Why did you do that?" she asked, as if she really did not know. "Why did you hurt me?"

When I didn't say anything she got up slowly, rubbing her arm where I had hit her, and then went over and sat down on the couch. Sat the way she had that first time, in the living room of her mother's house: knees together, back straight, hands folded in her lap, eyes cast down on her hands. She did not move; she did not even seem to be breathing.

Rapping on the door. And from out in the hallway Litchak yelled my name.

I called back, "You can come in now, Dennis, it's all over," and my voice sounded as if it were coming through liquid.

The door opened and he poked his white-maned head around the edge again. Came inside in tentative movements. He looked a little gray and shaken—but not nearly as gray and shaken as I felt.

"God Almighty," he said. He peered at me through his glasses, glanced over at Karen, looked back at me. "What the *hell* is going on?"

"It's a long story." I wanted to push away from the desk, go into the bedroom and get the phone and call Eberhardt; but I did not trust my legs just yet. "Listen, you probably saved my life. Thanks."

"I did?"

"You did. Why'd you come up? You hear me downstairs? Or was it your flat she buzzed to get in?"

"Neither one. I didn't even know you were home. I came up to check on the place again, like you asked me to, and saw the door standing open—"

A laugh popped out of me—sudden, humorless, ironic.

Litchak frowned. "What's funny?"

"Nothing," I said. "It's you showing up when you did."

"Huh?"

"Coincidence, Dennis. Just one more coincidence."

TWENTY-TWO

Four days passed. So did my cold, with some medical assistance from Doctor White and forty-eight hours in bed. And so did the worst of the nightmares about guns and water and death.

A number of things happened in those four days.

Item: Andy Greene was apprehended by Washington state officials trying to cross the border into Canada. In the suitcase he had with him were twenty-seven thousand dollars in cash and the Browning 9 mm automatic he had tried to use on me. He refused to talk to anyone except an attorney and was being held for extradition back to California.

Item: The Alcohol and Firearms investigators discovered a case of illicit whiskey hidden in Gus Kellenbeck's garage, along with certain evidence—nobody told me what it was—which broke the whole bootlegging operation wide open. The distillery turned out to be located on the British Columbia coast, near

Prince Rupert; it was raided by Canadian government agents and six other men were arrested. An eighth arrest was made, by the Federal boys a few miles down the coast from Bodega Bay, of a rancher whose barn had been used by Greene and Kellenbeck for storage. Still more arrests were expected on the trucking and distribution end.

Item: Karen Nichols had been charged with the murder of Christine Webster and the attempted murder of me and was being held in the psychiatric ward at San Francisco General. Neither Eberhardt nor anyone else in the Department had been able to talk to her; she went into a violent paranoid reaction each of the two times they tried.

Item: All charges against Martin Talbot were dropped, but he was still hospitalized for observation and treatment. He had not been told about his niece's arrest, of course; the doctors were afraid the news would destroy all chance for his recovery. But they were not optimistic anyway, according to Donleavy. Neither was I. Even if he did get better, what would he have to come home to, poor bastard?

Item: Laura Nichols was reported to be "in seclusion" with friends outside the city. She had made no effort to see her daughter, Eberhardt told me, nor had she gone back to visit her brother. Mourning for herself, probably, for her own shattered existence. Mourning the fact that insanity really did run in her family.

Item: The media gave me a lot of publicity and the phone rang several times—reporters asking questions and wanting to set-up interviews. One guy said he wanted to do a feature article on me and my pulp collection and what it was like to be a private eye. And would I pose for pictures wearing, you know, a trench-coat and a slouch hat? I told him I would think about it and that I would have my secretary, Effie Perine, get in touch with him. Literate guy that he was, he said he would look forward to Ms. Perine's call.

Item: I ate Thanksgiving dinner with Dennis Litchak and his wife, and the thanks I gave was that I was still alive. Afterward I told him I was going to buy him a case of Scotch for saving my arse as he had. He said hell, that wasn't necessary, but I insisted. Make it Johnnie Walker Black Label, he said.

Item: I went down to the office on Friday, my first day out since Tuesday's visit to Doctor White, and cleaned up the wreckage. Gave the slashed chair to Goodwill, along with the gouged and glue-damaged desk. Ordered replacements from a second-hand office-supply outfit. The place depressed me; it just did not feel the same any more. Maybe my CPA neighbor, Hadley, was right. Maybe it *was* time to think about moving out and setting up shop somewhere else.

On Saturday night Eberhardt and Donleavy and I went out for a steak dinner at a restaurant on Van Ness. It was the first chance we had had to get together—and both of them seemed to feel they owed me a meal.

"There's one thing that keeps gnawing at me," Eberhardt said over the first round of beers. "I can't seem to get it out of my mind."

"What's that?" I asked. "All the coincidence?"

"No, not exactly. It's what happened to those two families after their paths crossed—one of them wiped out completely, the other one just about wiped out in a different way."

"Yeah."

"I mean, Talbot and Victor Carding have an accident and it seems to trigger a chain reaction. Death on the one side, insanity on the other."

"It didn't quite start with the accident," Donleavy reminded him. "Other things happened before and at the same time."

"Sure," Eberhardt said. "That's part of it, too. As if . . . hell, I don't know, as if fate or something was out to get both families. As if all the coincidences weren't really coincidences at all. You know what I mean?"

I had never heard him sound so metaphysical; the thing was really bothering him, all right. But he was not alone. It bothered me a little, and Steve Farmer, judging from what he had said to me at Bodega Bay, and maybe Donleavy too.

"I know what you mean," I said.

"So how do you figure it?"

"You don't," Donleavy said. "You don't even want to try."

Silence for a time.

Eberhardt said finally, "The hell with it," and drained the last of his beer. "Let's have another round before we order."

"I've got a better idea," the last of the lone-wolf private eyes said. "Let's have three or four more rounds."

And we did.